Spirit *of the* Horse

THE NEW MYTHS OF EQUUS

Carole Devereux

Windhorse Press
Portland, OR

DEDICATION

I have devoted twenty years to raising awareness of the spiritual bond between humans and animals. I dedicate this book to those individuals, families, and animals I have met on my journey, who have helped me to find my way.

The Dignitary's Buddy

Tri-Ellie

Dutch

Judy Hudspeth

The Hunts Family

Thomas Wanzer Long

Jeri Ryan, Ph.D.

Penelope Smith

Dawn Baumann Brunke

Kelly King

Rosanne Bostonian, Ph.D.

Nancy Bantz

Christina Traunweiser

Michael O'Hern

Tristan Stark

The Buckler Family

Cover design: *White Horse of the Shamans* ~ Carole Devereux
Cover photograph: Jackie Robbins
Title art: Sandra Belfiore-Severson
Back cover photograph: Gregory A. Hunts

Published by Windhorse Press
40402 NE 74th Ave.
La Center, WA 98629

Library of Congress Cataloging-in-Publication Data
Control Number: 2009909689
Carole S. Devereux
Spirit of the Horse: The New Myths of Equus
Devereux, Carole S.
Spirit of the Horse: The New Myths of Equus
ISBN-1-884422-24-1
1. Animals 2. Spirituality

Buddy on Unicorns, printed with permission from the author.
Soft Moon Shining reprinted with permission from the author.

Praise for Carole Devereux
and
Spirit of the Horse

"This book truly is an offering to the spirit of the horse, to the earth, to the imaginative mind, and to the deep psyche. It has the feeling of a deep excavation of old and forgotten things. Carole Devereux has written a text that is boundless and deeply informative. It takes the reader all over the map, and then off it! It is a work of interspecies cultural restoration, and as such it works as a hybrid text--for which there are no conventional rules."

~ Tristan Stark, Poet/Editor
Graduate, Naropa University

"Carole Devereux's deep sensitivity and keen capacity convey to her students a clear path toward developing their animal communication skills. Carole provides support, knowledge and wisdom to create a setting of freedom and safety that allows her students to flourish. In her new book Carole and her horses provide myths that are in fact metaphors from which we can learn a great deal about combining spirituality with a right and compassionate way to take our Earth journey."

~ Dr. Jeri Ryan, Psychologist/Animal Communicator
Founder, Assisi International Animal Institute

Praise for Carole Devereux
and
Spirit of the Horse

"Carole Devereux brings us a book that bridges heart and mind, time and space to reunite us to our essential selves--longing for connection, longing to find our place in communion with horse and all the natural world. Both well-researched and well-inspired, this book is an invitation to another way of being with ourselves, our past, present, and our future, guided by the love and spirit of Horse."

Kate Solisti, author of *Conversations with Horse*
Fellow Animal Communicator and educator since 1992.

$(\approx$

"Carole Devereux, inspired by her deep connection with horses and her love of mythology, conveys a fascinating perspective about the spiritual nature of horses and communication with them. Absorbing her enlightened perspective will surely shift the old domineering way of relating to animals to a more sensitive, reverent, and loving treatment of them."

Penelope Smith, Founding Pioneer, Animal Communication Specialist and author, *When Animals Speak: Techniques for Bonding with Animal Companions, Animal Talk: Interspecies Communication,* and *Animals in Spirit: Our Faithful Companions' Transition to the Afterlife.*

§

*"There are days when
I hear your voice,
But today,
I hear your soul."*

Darlene Terry

CONTENTS

Section 1
Understanding Spiritual Power

Section 2
The Mythology of Equus: Part One

Section 3
The Mythology of Equus: Part Two
The Horse Goddess

Section 4
The Mythic Threshold:
Discovering Your Soul Myth

Section 5

Growing Your Potential for Animal Communication through Love, Joy Equanimity, and Compassion

ACKNOWLEDGMENTS

"At times our own light goes out and is rekindled by a spark from another person. Each of us has cause to think with deep gratitude of those who have helped to light the flame within us again."

~ Albert Schweitzer

Over the last fifteen years, there were often times when I thought this book was too overwhelming to finish. False starts, revisions, health care concerns, changes in residence and deaths in the family. These crises of growth seemed endless at the time. Yet, despite all of the trials, my friends, family, clients, students, teachers, and others I had met on the Internet encouraged me, rekindling my desire to serve the greater good with this project.

The best advice for sustaining writing over a long period I received from my horses—Buddy, Ellie, and Dutch. They are the true authors of this book, and I will always love them as my spiritual parents. Their advice was, "Always be in the present moment, and let the rest take care of itself."

My deepest gratitude goes to my dearest teachers, Dr. Jeri Ryan and Penelope Smith. They taught me how to be gentle with the power I hold in my heart when I am communicating with animals. They taught me that the moment I give my fullest attention to anything, even a blade of grass; it becomes a mysterious, awesome, magnificent world in itself. Learning to communicate with animals has helped me to communicate more deeply, more effectively, and more compassionately.

I want to thank my friend Tom Long for listening to me read the book aloud in his living room. His ideas kept me grounded. And, behind every good writer is a good editor, one who is honest and kind at the same time. For me, my editors fit that description---Dawn Baumann Brunke, Sabine Hilding, and Tristan Stark.

I also want to thank my best friend, Judy Hudspeth for her advice and sensitive wisdom when I was falling apart at the seams. Judy, you are a once-in-a-lifetime friend.

I would like to thank my husband, Greg, for his technical help when the computer crashed, threatening to erase everything I had ever written, and for supporting me when writing this book meant more than earning a living.

My sincere gratitude also goes to Adele Zimmerman for helping to write the guided visualizations, "Growing Your Potential for Animal Communication."

FOREWORD

By Penelope Smith

The field of animal communication has been rapidly expanding for over twenty years. Books on how to telepathically communicate with animals are widely available. Countless stories, photos, and video productions featured in the media show animals' intelligent communication, as well as their open-heartedness and compassion for one another and for humans. Scientific research validates the myriad "languages" of animals. All species behave in complex, purposeful, and intelligent ways.

As an animal communication specialist who has counseled thousands of people and their animal friends, I have seen that domesticated horses are one of the most exploited and misunderstood. When horses are treated as slaves to fulfill performance goals, humans can fail to notice and respect the intelligence of equines, their exquisite sensitivity, and spiritual qualities.

Carole Devereux, inspired by her deep connection with horses and her love of mythology, conveys a fascinating perspective about the spiritual nature of horses and communication with them. Absorbing her enlightened perspective will surely shift the old domineering way of relating to animals to a more sensitive, reverent, and loving treatment of them. Devereux brings us myths as spiritual treasures, leading us to be in the world with more compassion and awareness of the interconnectedness of all life. Myths communicated by humans and, in this book, horses, can help us find our way in the great energy interchange and drama of life.

Awareness of the depth of horse and all animal soul cannot be emphasized enough. It should be nurtured as vital for a true connection and understanding of both other species and our fellow humans, and as a path to discover our own true nature. When we feel and understand who animals really are, we feel and understand who we are. When we truly see other animals, looking into their eyes or otherwise feeling communion with them, we capture the essence of true relationship and oneness of all life. Animals' telepathic connection among themselves and with humans is then evident to us.

Be entranced by the poetic panorama the author unfolds, and feel renewed by the rolling breath of fresh air her book opens to us. Take the invitation offered here to revive within yourself the "Sacred Language of Spirit."

PREFACE

For all the words in our dictionaries, for all the dialects and languages we use to express our feelings and thoughts, for all the specialized jargon and poetic license we take, nothing is more powerful than mind-to-mind, telepathic communication.

Mind-to-mind telepathic communication is the experience of receiving the thoughts, ideas, feelings, emotions and mental imagery of other beings without the use of words, speech or body language. It is the direct transference of thought.

The *American Heritage Dictionary* defines telepathy as "communication by scientifically unknown or inexplicable means, as by the exercise of mystical powers." However, there is nothing mysterious or mystical about telepathic communication. It is much the same as invisible sound waves received by a radio, television, or telephone. The difference is that we are the sending and receiving mechanisms.

Just as a radio receives invisible sound waves, using a source, a medium, and a receiver, we can also receive and send messages using our minds and bodies. We often do it without being consciously aware of it. We receive telepathic messages from our spouses, children, friends, and even our animals. Some use the ability more than others, but we all have it at our disposal. Animals have the power to send and receive clear communication within their own species, called intraspecies communication. When humans and animals telepathically communicate, we call it interspecies communication.

After finding my horses in 1991, I discovered a deep telepathic bond existed between us, which led me to realize they had an abundance of spiritual wisdom to share with me. Through this telepathic process, we came to know a direct experience of the Divine together, and that is how this book was born.

Carole, Buddy, and Ellie

ABOUT THE AUTHOR

Born in the Hudson River Valley in 1951, and educated in New York, Carole Devereux (pronounced dev-er-o) started chronicling her life story at age eleven. Rediscovering those early diaries later in life revealed to her who she was as a young artist, author, and animal advocate.

As a teenager in 1969, Carole had a passion for the arts and pursued art history at Wagner College where she was also a conscientious objector during the Vietnam War. After two years at Wagner, Carole moved to Vermont to live on a commune before enrolling in the International Summer School at the University of Oslo, Norway where she studied interior architecture.

In the early 1970s, after traveling with friends through Norway and Western Europe, Carole settled in Paris to work as an Au Pair. She studied at Alliance Francaise and became fluent in French as she continued to write letters and short stories about her travels abroad.

After an extended stay in Paris, Carole picked up roots again and moved to Hollywood where she worked in the movie industry at Warner Bros, Paramount, and Columbia Studios as a script reader. It was there that she wrote her first script treatment, *Rainbow River*, about the adventures of a young Shaman and the legend of El Dorado in South America.

Thus, she began her writing career, circulating stories and scripts to major film studios.

In the mid 1980s, Carole attended the Healing Light Center in Los Angeles, directed by Rosalyn Bruyere. After rigorous testing, the school accepted Carole into their advanced healing program, affectionately called the "God Squad." The training she acquired in energy awareness there eventually led to her love of telepathic animal communication.

In 1993, Carole's interest in communicating with her horses, Buddy, Ellie, and Dutch, inspired her to study with Penelope Smith and Dr. Jeri Ryan, the leading pioneers in the field of interspecies communication. After years of training, Carole began to sponsor Dr. Ryan's Basic and Advanced Animal Communication Workshops in Portland, Oregon. These workshops helped to raise funds for the Assisi International Animal Institute, founded by Dr. Ryan in 1995. Carole also produced a three-hour audio lecture titled *Telepathic Communication: A Compassionate Journey* featuring Dr. Jeri Ryan.

In 1994, Carole traveled again to southern France, this time to study the cave paintings at Lascaux, Niaux, Font-de-Gaume, and others near Les Eyzies in the Dordogne Valley. It was there that she discovered the important purpose that Paleolithic cave art, animal communication, and Shamanism would play in her spiritual journey, and in writing this book.

During 1997, Carole started her own animal communication consulting practice, Animal Insights. She continues to teach, consult, and mentor students nationwide. She wrote and self-published her first book, a regional best seller, *The NW Oregon Stable Guide: 100 Boarding, Breeding, and Training Stables for Horses*, to help horse owners locate the perfect home for their horses in the Pacific Northwest.

Carole lives with her husband, Gregory Hunts, an Information Center Manager at a Portland law firm. They live in rural Washington on a 10-acre property with their horses, cats, and dogs. To reach Carole Devereux please visit her website at www.animalinsights.com.

Ellie and Buddy at home in Washington

DANCING WITH A PRINCE

When I was seven years old and living with my parents in New York, my brother and I begged our mother to let us have a puppy. We were so happy when we found a little mutt that looked like a German Shepherd. We thought he was adorable and we named him Prince.

I felt I understood what Prince needed, and I knew he understood me too. One day, our mother decided she did not want Prince anymore, and she told us that Prince was going away. Then, while we were at school, she called the local shelter. They came, picked him up, and took him to the shelter, some 20 miles away.

Later that week, maybe exactly one week, we were sitting in the living room when we heard something scratching at the back door. When we went to see who was there, we were amazed to find it was Prince. He was thin, but he seemed okay. We were so happy he was home with us again. A child's heart is so deeply bonded to animals at that age.

I still remember the look on my mother's face. She marched into the living room and called the shelter. "How is our dog Prince doing?" she asked. I recall her laughter when they told her, "Prince is doing just fine." She replied, "Yes, he is doing so fine that he is on our back porch." After what I assume were profuse apologies, they said someone would be right over to get him.

The truth is that Prince, who was only one or two years old at the time, had jumped over the fence at the shelter and found his way back to our house. It had taken him a week traveling on dangerous highways without food or water. When we realized what he had done, we pleaded with our mother to let us keep him. But she returned Prince to the shelter that day, and we never saw him again.

This is one of many animal stories that have stayed in my mind and heart over the years. These are the deeper memories that motivate us, as adults, to continue to advocate for animals, even against the most difficult odds.

Carole and Prince ~ 1958

Introduction: My Spiritual Journey

"It is important for modern people to find their mythic roots and regain their lost sense of spiritual connectedness to the universe."

The Mythic Imagination:
Your Quest for Meaning Through Personal Mythology

~ Stephen Larsen, Ph.D.

This book is the joyful unfolding of a collective effort between humans and animals. The aim? To establish greater compassion and awareness of the spiritual connection that humanity shares with all of nature–plants, animals, rocks, and a myriad of spiritual beings.

It is written with the view that nature and animals can enlighten, guide, and help humans to restore a lost chord of sacred truth and meaning in our lives. This work is a meditation on a deep, very old dream that I have been nurturing for many lifetimes. It is the fulfillment of a promise that I made to myself to work to alleviate animal suffering, especially for horses, all over the world.

I made this promise after seeing how humans have exploited horses as beasts-of-burden for so many centuries. I wanted to help horses experience a sense of spiritual freedom, to balance the suffering they have endured. Only since the rediscovery of telepathic, interspecies communication in the last two decades, have horses been able to proclaim their truths as living symbols of spiritual freedom to the world.

In the early 1990s, I began to realize my long-held dream when I married my husband, Greg, and we moved to a 16-acre hilltop property in Portland, Oregon. At the time, my dream for horses was still embedded in my unconscious mind. Looking back, I realize it has taken more than a decade to excavate this dream from the depths of my soul. After what seems like many lifetimes (in this lifetime it has been fifteen years) working toward this end, I am just now beginning to realize fully the meaning of my spiritual journey with animals.

I found my first horse, Buddy, in 1990. He reignited my passion for helping horses. We agreed that Buddy would be my guardian spirit, teacher, ally, and protector. He would act as a support for my spiritual healing. Buddy had already been broken to ride, yet still had a fair amount of wildness left in him. In return, I promised to help him realize his ambition to improve life on Earth for all beings, which then became our combined destiny: To write books about the secret, spiritual life of horses.

One day, Buddy told me that he had come to the Earth to establish an organization from the ground up, a sort of "grass roots," (yes, pun intended) organization. He wanted to write books about interspecies communication. Buddy wanted humans to expand their views of communication, and to inspire us to open our minds and hearts to understanding and learning from nature. Buddy said, "Every breath we take is a communication with the air. What would the air want us to know about our bodies? Where is the air stuck inside of us? Where does it sense we need more of it? What does the air want us to know about its relationship with us? If we follow the path of air into our bodies, personify it and give it a voice, we will find the information it has to share."

I got to know Buddy while taking lessons and training him on the trails around our house. But when he was injured by another horse at his boarding stable, I asked my husband to build a barn on our property so I could bring Buddy home.

 After a year with us, I felt Buddy was lonely for another horse. So I asked him if he would like a same-species partner. He pictured a beautiful, wild-spirited, white Arabian mare with flowing mane and tail. At the time, I was too new to the horse world to think of taming such a wild thing. So I asked again. "Do you have anyone else in mind?" Instantly, he projected an image of a dark bay Thoroughbred. Within a few weeks I had found Ellie who then became his lifetime mate.

Immediately upon seeing each other they were both impassioned. It took some time for them to sort out their differences---Ellie wanted nothing less than the role of alpha mare, which Buddy finally allowed. And when they began to trust each other completely, they never parted again.

I began to write this book with their help and the guidance of my mentors and invisible teachers in the supernatural realms. We wrote it with the wish that others will enjoy the secret, intimate view of what Buddy calls, "The Spiritual Life of Horses."

Although it was Buddy's idea to write a book, over the years I became more committed to discovering and exploring animal spirituality. It became my passion to join other voices

26

around the world in a chorus of celebration for the combined, evolving consciousness of humanity and the species Equus.

For thousands of years, the horse has been an inspiring and persuasive mythological icon. When exalted, their indomitable spirits rise from the depths of an untold dream, perhaps conjured by a fantasy to fly, spiraling up from the ashes, like the Phoenix, soaring into the light of new millenniums. The mythology of the horse is, therefore, the dream of the horse. As such, these myths are made from the same mind-stuff.

Another calling I began to recognize was to bring out of the undifferentiated mind stream of divine consciousness, the birthplace of all dreams and myths, an enlightened mythical narrative for horses so that they could realize a mystical and mythological Renaissance. Freeing their consciousness in this way is a breakthrough no captive beast would hesitate to embrace.

Therefore, this book weaves many different voices and threads throughout its pages. At first it may appear linear, but look again. The book is deeply, multi-layered. You can pick it up and open it at random to find new meaning, depending on your state of mind. There are many levels in each section. Each chapter is a reflection of the whole, similar to a hologram.

My wish is that the book will inspire other artists and writers to explore the myriad of myths that nonhuman species wish to tell. This process will unleash creative minds and unify the collective wisdom inside the matrix of life.

Section 1

Understanding Spiritual Power

CHAPTER ONE

Spirit Primer:
Definition of Terms

Man's laws change with his understanding of man. Only the laws of the spirit remain always the same.

~ Crow Proverb

What can humans learn about spirit from a horse? That is what this book is about. So that readers may understand what Buddy meant by the term "spirit" in the title of the book, I have written a Spirit Primer to provide a basic understanding of the subject.

Many readers will likely be familiar enough with the subject of spirituality to know how I have used the word. But for those who would like clarification, you will find a Judeo-Christian description of the word, as well as various indigenous views on the subject.

All in all, it is my wish that readers from all walks of life will find the Spirit Primer enlightening, and that you will continue to discover your own experience of what spirit means to you.

What's in a Word?

Every word has a story behind it. In English we call the study of the derivation of words etymology. Etymology teaches us how and when a word first came into expression. According to the online *Merriam-Webster Dictionary*, the word, "etymology" was introduced in the 14th century from two Greek words: *etymon*, meaning "truth" and *logia*, meaning "the study of." Thus, etymology refers to the study of the "true origins of words."

Etymology explores the history and development of a linguistic form from its earliest recorded occurrences. By tracking its distribution from one language to another and by identifying related words in other languages, we can find a common ancestral form in an ancestral language.

Anyone who finds language interesting may enjoy the study of words. Nearly one-third of all English words are descended from Latin or Greek roots, or from Old English and Germanic roots. Words may be borrowed from other languages too, such as the word "alligator." It entered the English language because of a contact between English and Spanish speakers in Florida. In Spanish, "alligator" is el *ligarto*--the lizard. As the English borrowed this Spanish word, they changed it into its modern English form.

Each of us knows that personal experiences color and define the way we use words. As a teacher of interspecies communication, I emphasize the importance of experiencing feelings more fully to appreciate the deeper truths of the soul. I often ask my students to hold their verbalization to a minimum during an animal communication workshop. The reason is that many students are overwhelmed when they try to put their deeper emotions into words. Words often fall short of true meaning and real exchange. We may also use words to justify or distance ourselves or to disguise our true feelings.

Over the years, I have found that animals use fewer words in their communications with humans than humans use with each other. Animals communicate with humans using pictures, feelings, and behaviors as much as, or more than, they use words. In this way, animals help us to reach into our deepest, most vital emotions and bring them to the surface.

In his book, *Soulcraft*, Bill Plotkin identifies sacred speech as "a conversation that deepens relationships and enhances the fullness of our presence wherever we are and whomever we are with." He further advises that, "an effective strategy for tuning awareness to the frequency of soul is to minimize everyday conversation that separates us from here and now and from what is truly meaningful."

In order to understand human language, we need to organize patterns of words into a cohesive whole for meaning. Animals often use pictures to communicate their thoughts and feelings to humans. These pictures contain symbols that the brain recognizes instantly. Symbols bypass the analytical brain and go straight to the intuitive, right brain hemisphere.

Words often do not address our inner conflicts at the deepest levels of consciousness. Talking can be therapeutic, but genuine feelings must accompany conversation. Words that do not point to real experience do not lead to understanding. Excessive talk only reinforces anxiety and obliterates the authentic self, the self that teaches and heals at the unconscious level.

According to Buddhist philosophy, 'Right Speech' is sacred speech that occurs when we say the right thing at the right time and when what we say is useful and truthful. Speech is like a treasure when uttered in the perfect moment. It can take a poet, writer or lyricist years to hone the craft of expressing these deeper emotions artfully.

Buddy once advised a student, "Shut up and listen to your Self." Now that may not have been artfully spoken, but it was intended as therapeutic advice, and characteristic of Buddy. What he meant was, "get out of your head and into your heart." This is how we experience the sacred, pre-verbal world of the inner child. When we listen at this profound level, we can hear what is going on 'at the heart' of things. Buddy says, "It is only when we are aware of what is really going on inside (underneath the words) that we can alter the outside world." When we do not listen at this level, Buddy calls it, "talking over your Self." Listening at this level helps us to access the emotional body that was laid in place before we acquired language skills as children. In psychology, this is sometimes called the "unthought known." It is the core of the self that is nonverbal and unconscious and is the basis of the developing self in childhood.

Often my students ask if human communication is not contradictory to the ways nonhumans think and communicate (because humans have such complex patterns of speech). The answer is yes. Yet, it is also true that humans share the same ground of deeper awareness with nonhumans. It is during this profound communication with the core self, that co-creative spiritual expression really flourishes between species. This kind of communication comes from the heart, not the intellect. We will go deeper into the pre-verbal world of our ancestors as they communicated with each other and nature telepathically in the following chapters.

In Chapter Fifteen, we explore the meaning of co-creative spiritual expression and how to awaken creativity by following simple, guided exercises designed to help readers achieve greater spiritual clarity. The purpose is to experience spirituality and creativity as inseparable.

Through another series of visualizations, we delve into the inner self to unearth our soul myths. This method of self discovery helps us to understand the importance of soul-to-soul contact when learning how to communicate with nonhuman nature.

Is Spirit Synonymous with Religion?

The two words, spirit and religion, are often considered equivalent. But are they? *Webster's Collegiate Dictionary* traces the word religion back to an old Latin word, *religio*, meaning "taboo or restraint." A deeper study reveals the word comes from two words, *re* and *ligare*. *Re* is a prefix that means, "to return" and *ligare* means, "to bind." In other words, religion means, "to return to bondage." I find it interesting that Buddy did not title his book, *Religion of the Horse*. When I asked him about the word spirit he simply said, "You can replace the word spirit with the word love." When I asked him about the word religion he said, "Humans have invented religion to house their collective soul, but the spirit is free and cannot be contained inside a religion."

Thousands of years ago, humans were more intuitively and spiritually based. Today, we have shifted toward economically and politically based societies. Religious temples, once at the center of our villages, have been replaced by monolithic financial towers. Perhaps this movement toward materialism explains why so many have so much difficulty maintaining a spiritual focus. Do we find it hard to find time for a spiritual path because we have too many possessions to maintain?

Family Values: A Spiritual Imperative

"When a family declines, ancient traditions are destroyed. With them the spiritual foundations for life are forfeited, and the family loses its sense of unity. Where there is no sense of unity, the women of the family can become corrupted. With the corruption of women, society plunges into chaos." ~ Bhagavad Gita: 1:40

Many people feel alienated today because they are not emotionally or spiritually bonded to family and community. Our technological and industrial societies, although advanced, have produced generations of children and adults who are skilled in finance and politics but uninitiated into the spiritual side of life. Instead of family rituals, initiations, and ceremonies, adolescents risk everything while taking drugs and facing their own death or causing harm to others. Perhaps these extreme measures are tantamount to the risks their souls would have asked them to experience in more meaningful ways, i.e., rituals or rites of passage. Since we do not generally venerate our elders in American society today, these rites of passage are not being passed down to younger generations.

Everyone needs to feel a part of something bigger than themselves. We need to feel valued for our spiritual legacies, our monetary worth, and our technological skills. But this requires that we know and experience ourselves as sacred beings. Organized religion tried to accomplish this goal in the past, but we are not following the dictates of the church as much as we once did. One way to experience our lives as sacred is through pure insight and through our myths and stories of origin. In this book, we address the finer aspects of spirit through the process of creation mythology.

Naming the Unnameable

Now, let us look at a few definitions of spirit from an American dictionary, and then consider it from the Old Testament. I included several indigenous or Native American perspectives on this subject as well. I like the Native North American approach because over the years Native American spirituality has helped me to align my own spiritual beliefs with the study of animal communication.

The etymology of the word spirit leads back to the ancient word for 'breath' or 'wind' or 'air.' It stems from the Latin *spirare*, meaning to breathe. The *Merriam-Webster* online dictionary defines spirit as the vital principle or animating force within living beings, as incorporeal consciousness. Spirit can mean Holy Spirit, "Holy" meaning pure. The word spirit can also mean a supernatural being, such as an angel or demon, and it can refer to a being that inhabits or embodies a particular place, object, or natural phenomenon, such as a fairy or a sprite. Spirit can also mean the essential nature of a person, place, group, or thing.

For the purposes of this book, I support the definition of spirit as "the essential divine nature of a person, place or thing." I include animals in this definition because I know animals also have souls.

Therefore, the word spirit means essence. It is the essence of a living being, person, place or thing. Spirit is the essential invisible animating principle that goes beyond physical manifestation in the microcosmic world.

The Meaning of Spirit in the Old Testament

All cultures hold their own beliefs about spirit. The Hebrew term for spirit is *ruah*. The Latin word is *spiritus,* both meaning breath. Breath is the most intangible reality anyone can know. Our hands cannot grasp it; yet we understand it is vitally important. Those who do not breathe do not live.

The Hebrew *ruah,* just as the Latin *spiritus,* designates the movement of the wind. We do not see the wind and yet we feel its presence. From observing the invisible, powerful wind, the ancients came to regard it as the "spirit of God." In both the Old and New Testaments the word passes easily from one meaning to the other. To help Nicodemus understand the way the Holy Spirit performed, Jesus used the comparison of the wind, and employed the same term in both cases: "The wind blows wherever it pleases . . . That is how it is with all who are born of the Wind (i.e., of the Holy Spirit)." John 3:8. Psalm 33:6: "By the word of the Lord were the heavens made, and all the host of them by the breath of his mouth."

The main idea expressed in the biblical word spirit is not of an intellectual power, but that of a dynamic impulse, similar to the force of the wind. In the Bible, the primary function of spirit is not to give understanding, but to give *movement,* not to shed light, but to impart dynamism. This can also be applied to the horse born to run free. So the *Spirit of the Horse* can refer to the movement of the horse, or the freedom of movement that horses enjoy, or the action of the horse in a spiritual sense.

Native American Views of Spirit

To explore Native American spirituality as a single entity for understanding the meaning of the word 'spirit' would be misleading. More than one thousand Native tribes lived in North America when the first Europeans arrived. Each tribe had its own set of festivals, rituals, ceremonies, spiritual beliefs, and practices. Yet many common features existed between tribal traditions.

Spirituality played a central role in the lives of these people, as author Angie Debo writes in her book, *A History of the Indians of the United States*: "He [the Indian] was deeply religious. The familiar shapes of Earth, the changing sky, the wild animals he knew, were joined with his own spirit in mystical communion. The powers of nature, the personal quest of the soul, the acts of daily life, the solidarity of the tribe--all were religious, and were sustained by dance and ritual."

A Mysterious Presence

Vine Deloria, Jr., scholar and winner of the 2003 American Indian Festival of Words Author Award for his book, *Spirit and Reason*, writes about the mysterious energy that affects all living things. "Native and tribal peoples experience and intuit, underneath the multitude of physical entities in the natural world, the presence of a mysterious, personal energy. One tribe may call it Orenda, another Puha, a third Manitou. All imply the same energy, but with a hint of personality."

Native peoples may describe this energetic presence in words but, unlike western religions, they do not define its substance or meaning. In fact, they resist pronouncing the sacred name of the mysterious energy, and use only the language of allusion and indirect speech to refer to it.

Manifestations

According to Deloria, the mysterious, personal energy is confined to a single physical form for a limited or more or less finite period on Earth. Since the physical life of beings includes suffering, the person's spirit helps the person find his/her way back home to the Great Mystery. This process suggests that suffering may increase or decrease in direct proportion to one's awareness and connection to the mysterious energy or to what we call God.

Deloria notes that during the historical journey that Native Americans have made upon the Earth, various personalities have emerged to represent the dominant expressions of this mysterious universal power. These personalities are not "gods" in the traditional Judeo-Christian sense. Instead, the personalities are endowed with a sacredness that contrasts with the material world. Native Americans describe these personalities as spirits who have roles in the creation and continuation of the universe.

Each entity helps to make up the natural world and takes a part in the mysterious energy. All the entities are equal in the sense that all share custody of the Earth together. No one alone has more or less value. Native Americans put less emphasis on worshiping, and more on petitioning spirits for help. Their ceremonies focus on petitions and thanksgivings for support from the spiritual world.

Consensual Spiritual Intention

Deloria tells us that there are some basic requirements for Native American rituals. One is that all creatures are allowed to attend all ceremonies, and that they cannot transform natural objects without the specific instructions or permission from the spirit of that object. To do anything else would violate the integrity of the entity. The use of any natural object must conform to the original purpose of the object. An example is their treatment of peyote for religious purposes. Native Americans do not alter peyote, for example, since it is a violation of the spirit of the plant. Native Americans are cautious with the essence of the plant. They regard the processing of plants for their chemical derivatives an act of disrespect. Everything in the physical world has its own integrity and that the task of spiritual practitioners is to create a minimum of disruption while performing ceremonial functions.

Immanence – To Remain Within

Native American spirituality centers on the idea that everything is naturally endowed with a spirit and that a constant social and spiritual exchange occurs among all of creation. To function with integrity, we need to appreciate and be cautious with the spirits of Fire, Air, Earth, and Water. Everything has its own divine purpose. Consciousness is not only the province of human beings in the Native American worldview, but that of all life. Winona La Duke, a member of the Green Party who ran with Ralph Nader in 2000, and a well-known advocate for Native American and women's issues, explains in her book, *The Winona LaDuke Reader: A Collection of Essential Writings:*

"According to our way of looking at things, the world is animate. We reflect this in our language, in that most nouns are animate . . . Natural things are alive and they have a spirit. Therefore, when we harvest wild rice on our reservations we offer tobacco to the Earth because, when you take something, you must give thanks to its spirit for giving itself to you."

John Mohawk, who died in 2006, was a leading scholar and representative for the Six Nations Iroquois Confederacy. He was an advocate for the rights of the Iroquois people. Mohawk eloquently expressed the indigenous relationship to creation when he wrote in his book, *Exiled in the Land of the Free: Democracy, Indian Nations, and the U.S. Constitution:*

"The natural world is our bible. We do not have chapters and verses; we have trees and fish and animals. The creation is the manifestation of energy through matter. Because the universe is made up of manifestations of energy, the options for that manifestation are infinite. But we have to admit that the way it has manifested itself is organized. In fact, it is the most intricate organization. We cannot know how we impact its laws; we can only talk about how its laws affect us. We make no judgments about nature. The Indian sense of natural law is that nature informs us and it is our obligation to read nature as we would a book, to feel nature as we would a poem, to touch nature as we would ourselves, and to be a part of it, and step into its cycles as much as possible."

All My Relations

Mitakuye Oyasin: We are all Related

~ Lakota Sioux Prayer

"All My Relations" is a phrase that many Native Indians use as an opening invocation and closing blessing for their spiritual ceremonies. This statement means "we are of one spirit" and that we need to respect the living spirit in other beings. It is through this common spirit that we are all joined. In other words, Indians have learned that by observing and communicating with animals and nature, and with the "living spirit" in nature, that the success of life on Earth is based on respect. Native Americans understand that ecological systems survive best as a single, unified whole. This includes plants, animals, humans, and elements. Joseph Epes Brown, author of *Teaching Spirits: Understanding Native American Religious Traditions*, writes:

"Running through nearly all indigenous Native American traditions is the pervasive theme that the sacred mysteries of creation are communicated to humans through all forms and forces of the immediately experienced natural environment. Such openness of mind and being, toward manifestations of the sacred, has made it possible for Native Americans to adopt the Christian expression of values into the fabric of their own religious culture."

Extinction as Myth

"When one tugs at a single thing in nature, he finds it attached to the rest of the world."
~ John Muir

It is an old Indian medicine teaching that plants and animals do not become extinct, but their spirits go away and do not come back until the location or habitat is again treated with the proper spiritual respect. Land abused for generations, if treated with spiritual respect, will see a flowering again. Some may think they are extinct, but birds and animals related to those plants also return. It is worth noting that plants return first, then the animals, and then finally the birds. Thus, antelope have returned to some portions of the Dakota plains, but prairie chickens have still not made a complete return.

Because all life is connected to each other, we not only pass our knowledge to other humans, we also pass our knowledge to all of creation. In this way, insight and moral power pass freely between species on Earth.

Spirit and Native American Creation Myths

Because this book highlights equine creation myths, as they relate to the spiritual life of horses, let us look for a moment at how the idea of the human spirit has been cultivated through creation myths from the ancient past.

In Native American mythology two features stand out in contrast to Judeo-Christian creation myths: First, the idea of original sin resulting in being cast out of the place to which one is born does not exist in Native American spirituality. Second, in Native American mythology there is no "Kingdom of Heaven" awaiting us on the other side as our 'true' spiritual home. Native Americans do not believe they have been locked out of the Garden of Eden. Their myths confirm that (unless they have been displaced by European contact and settlement) Native Americans live in the place intended by the Great Spirit, either at the site of their own emergence or by creation, or in a 'Promised Land' attained through long migration.

Native Americans experience the Earth as their homeland. First, the 'Kingdom of Heaven' is happening right now, not in a mythical place in the future. The Earth is not a weigh station on the way to some heavenly home. Native American creation myths portray a different understanding about the place we occupy, vis-à-vis animal, plant and mineral co-inhabitants. Native Americans believe that rather than humans having 'supremacy' over these life forms, animals, plants, and minerals are their companions, from whom they learn the ways of the Great Mystery.

Native American myths and stories stress mutuality, interdependence, and esteem between people and other creatures. Mutual respect is needed when interacting with trees, birds, plants, and the natural forces--the four elements and the four directions.

Their myths inform Native Americans that creation is an ongoing process and that "All That Is" is a part of an ongoing creation story. For them, the spirit that infuses the world has not stopped existing and is simply experienced as 'immanence,' the spirit that imbues all things.

Energy & Spirit Interchangeable

Deloria suggests that the word 'energy' can be substituted for the word 'spirit.' Einstein's theory of energy/matter reveals that matter and energy are different forms of the same thing, and that matter can be turned into energy and energy into matter. The equation E is equal to M C-squared, in which energy is equal to mass, multiplied by the square of the velocity of light, shows that small amounts of mass can be converted into large amounts of energy and vice versa. The first tangible evidence of this was the atomic bomb detonated in New Mexico on July 16, 1945.

What if we exchanged the word spirit for the word energy, does it still relate to Einstein's discovery? A question to ponder is this: Did our collective lack of spiritual consciousness, or collective memory-loss regarding our divine energy (spirit) become the grounds for creating an atomic bomb that could destroy the world? What if we replace the word 'energy' with the word 'spirit' in Einstein's equation. How does the meaning change?

Albert Einstein understood that his formula might lead to destruction someday, and although he was a peaceful man, he urged the President to fund his research before Germany or Japan developed their bombs. The result was the Manhattan Project that produced the first evidence of Einstein's research. It was one of the greatest ironies that Einstein, a pacifist, helped to initiate the era of nuclear weapons.

One focus of this book is to help readers realize the forces of the human spirit and the forces in nature, including animals, are equal to the powerful forces of a nuclear bomb. So, can we conclude that whoever controls these forces, controls the world?

Using the connection we have to spirit, the powerful life force that animates all living things, can we create a force that goes against nature and becomes potentially lethal? Or, if used soundly, can our conscious spiritual awareness, used with love and compassion, strengthen our collective integrity enough to heal the Earth, her creatures and humanity as a whole? It is our choice. But first, we must become informed.

CHAPTER TWO

Ancestor Horse

"We now know that there is not one space and one time only, but as many spaces and times as there are subjects, as each subject is contained within its own environment that possesses its own space and time."

Theoretical Biology

~ Jacob van Uexkull

Roughly sixty million years ago, primitive horses embarked upon a long and arduous journey across the face of this vast Earth. By studying their fossil remains scientists have learned what prehistoric life must have been like for these noble creatures. Insight into the world of the modern horse today would be incomplete without some knowledge of their prehistory.

In the following pages, we will observe a small band of early horses, as seen through the lens of their own eyes. The power of the extraordinary spirit of the horse lies deep within their ancestral past. Inside this story is a message of appreciation for all God's creatures. We need to revere them, not only for their strength and power, but also as creatures of miraculous spirit and grace.

Created or Evolved?

When we concern ourselves with the natural history of life on Earth, are we disavowing God? That may be hard to answer for many people. And keeping all these ideas in balance between science and religion can be difficult.

This book reflects the idea that all life on Earth embodies divine consciousness, whether created or evolved, and that we can tap into this consciousness and bring it to the surface of awareness at anytime. This was apparent to me when I first started sharing my own consciousness with the consciousness of my horses. Sharing divine awareness between species has helped me to realize my highest spiritual potential. The animals have revealed the inspiration that we share with them as co-creators with God and nature.

Should We Fear Extinction?

Although extinctions on Earth may be a natural outcome of the seemingly infinite cycles of life, scientists have confirmed that the current rate of extinctions is accelerating dramatically. The more we know and accept the consequences (which we share with other life forms in keeping the balance of life on Earth intact) the more we realize that the Earth, the animals, and us, the humans, depend on one another for survival. It is an enormous challenge for us to give up the way we live to protect animals and the Earth from destruction. Yet, if we honor the messages that are being conveyed to those who will listen about the Earth from our nonhuman companions, we can meet this challenge with confidence.

In the book, *The Soul of Nature: Celebrating the Spirit of the Earth*, edited by Michael Tobias and Georgianne Cowan, Joseph Bruchac notes, "Our lack of understanding of the spirituality of all life, of the great mysterious spirit in nature that we must respect, is at the root of our current environmental crisis."

While learning the ways of ancient life on Earth, as viewed through the eyes and spirits of horses in these pages, we will gain a sharper insight into how Mother Nature deals with new equilibriums. Since we are inextricably tied to the Earth, when the Earth's experiences change, we are all affected. If we humans can accept these ideas, we can allow our collective spirit to teach us about the natural laws of the Earth and the animals. Our science has come to a greater understanding of the natural world and the processes that make it function. Now we need to listen and honor those processes because they are important to our collective survival.

In *Last Cry: Native American Prophesies*, Robert Wolf notes that we must relearn how to live with the Earth. "It is time to honor Spirit. It is time to listen to Earth-Mother-Goddess. Learn to listen with your heart. If you learn this, you will know the wisdom of the ages. Allow, allow, allow. Earth is feminine, a Goddess."

Our journey then will be a discovery process of the unified consciousness that we share with one another, the Earth, and the animals. Knowledge of this shared essence lies awaiting discovery, deep within the core of each being.

Deep Time Travel

Is time real? Since we are going to explore what I call "deep time" with horses, I thought it would be appropriate to expound a bit on the idea of time travel. Time is a concept relative to awareness. As we explore different levels in different periods or epochs in this chapter, we will forget our present time and descend into parallel dimensions for better understanding, and sometimes healing.

The unconscious mind is a portal for time travel as well as an entrance into other dimensions. If we can calibrate the conscious mind to alpha waves, we can activate this portal. While visiting other dimensions during time travel, third dimensional time is forgotten or dissolved until the multidimensional traveler returns from his or her journey.

The conscious mind on the other hand is the great integrator of experiences in all dimensions. It absorbs many messages from the unconscious, the higher consciousness, or Christ consciousness, while simultaneously being aware of routine physical reality. That is possible because consciousness expands like light. It expands into higher dimensions as well as into lower dimensions. In the following pages, we will travel back through deep time to view the prehistory of the horse through this other-dimensional time portal.

Eocene Epoch: A Hot House Jungle

For modern humans, the extinct dinosaurs are the most popular ancient creatures. However, for me, a more interesting species is the one that survived extinction some 11,000 years ago in North America. That is the ever-adaptable species Equus.

As we turn back the clock to the Eocene, we are immersed in the flow of geological time. Fifty-five million years ago, the Earth was rich with many now extinct species. As you may know, *Eo* means dawn, and *cene* means recent. We are on what is called the North American continent. Dinosaurs have been extinct for about ten million years, and the remaining mammals are growing larger and becoming more diverse.

Let us imagine we are walking amid a grove of ancient, tall cypress trees towering above a thick, equatorial jungle. Profuse tropical vines, laced throughout the upper story, filter warm sunlight onto the moist ground below. Juicy orange mangoes and luscious, heart-shaped custard apples droop heavily from their branches. We hear the sound of screeching birds overhead. It becomes obvious that all who share in this bounty, grandeur, and abundance, share in it equally.

Our footsteps fall lightly on leafy green ferns and low-lying shrubs; we press deeper into the jungle. At times, we sink into soggy marshland. The intoxicating fragrance of magnolias mixed with the pungent odor of camphor, fills the air. It is a balmy evening and the luxuriant atmosphere elevates our senses.

 The ancestral animals in this prehistoric realm enjoy a healthy, happy existence. In spite of some physical differences they all have one thing in common: They are warm-blooded, air-breathing mammals. Other species are also recognizable, such as reptiles, crocodiles, turtles, and frogs. Many plant-eating mammals are swinging in the treetops, out of harm's way, and a few smaller mammals are browsing quietly in the underbrush on tender,

fresh leaves, nuts, and roots.

Among this colorful menagerie, we see a swiftly moving creature darting past us. He seems on the alert for something in the wind. This prehistoric beast is one that scientists now call *Hyracotherium*. His popular name is *Eohippus*, meaning Dawn Horse.

He is a novel creature compared with modern horses. He walks on four toes on his front feet and three toes on his back feet. His legs are less flexible but lighter and more loosely gaited than later horses. While running, he bears his weight on elevated under pads.

The herd favors females over males two to one. An individual *Eohippus* male enjoys a harem of several females for most of his life. Although the size of an ancient herd of *Eohippus* is average compared with other animal herds in the forest, their herd size increases significantly during their heyday in the Miocene Epoch—some 23.8 to 5.3 million years ago.

These small horses have brindled fur and pointed snouts, with little erect ears. Their close-set eyes are set midway in their skulls, unlike today's horses whose eyes are set back and to the sides. Dawn Horses can easily dart over logs and branches because of their high rounded backs and muscled haunches, which provide swifter movement than modern Equus.

A shower of warm rain drenches us and we run for cover under a nearby cypress tree. Just after the monsoon begins, it stops abruptly, and groups of small horses band together at the river's edge to exchange reports of their communal domain.

In the distance, a bubbling swamp, filled with murky compost, creates an ominous backdrop. The animals begin by trading stories of the dangers they have experienced. If we become very still, we can listen to the stories they are communicating to one another . . . telepathically.

Let us focus on a brindled female from a herd of twenty horses who is browsing on leaves and shoots. She watches over her two young babies as they walk toward the river. She leads them to a bush and tells one to stay while she takes the other one to drink. As she lowers her head, she tells her baby to watch and listen carefully. In the distance, another female surveys the grove for them. The mother motions her baby to drink while she sends pictures and feelings of potential predators that may be hiding in the darkness. She tells her baby to listen far into the distance while teaching her to be alert with all of her senses. These small horses are prey animals and easily killed when they drink in the open. The youngest horse takes a drink and projects that she wants to go into the water. But her mother nudges her back onto the shore, and they return to the herd.

When they arrive, the male stallion in charge of the harem is showing the others he has been injured. He is dragging his bleeding hind leg. He projects a huge bird with sharp claws and flesh ripping beak, warning the others of the fearsome creature that attacked him.[1] The stallion alerts the females not to travel north. They are alarmed, prancing about, but all agree. The stallion tells them he escaped only because he fought hard; they will need to be careful to protect their young tonight.

---

[1]*Diatryma*, courtesy of Oberlin College.

One female takes the stallion to wash his wounds in the river. As the sun sets, the herd looks for night cover. The females shelter their young while they sleep. At dawn the harem is saddened to learn that their stallion has died during the night from his injuries. The mares, preoccupied with thoughts of finding a new leader by nightfall, leave the area with their infants close behind.

Thus, we see an example of the challenges early horses endured millions of years ago. Without the ability to communicate telepathically through intraspecies communication, these species would likely not have survived into the present day.

 Now, we see another group of early horses interacting with primitive creatures in the Eocene jungle. These horses have just felt an unwanted guest lurking in their domain. They become spooked as they dart for cover into a dark thicket. The smallest animals also scurry back and forth looking for a safe place to hide. Suddenly, the smell of citrus fills the air as a huge beast lazily appears from behind a cypress tree. He nonchalantly drops a piece of fruit onto the ground as he lumbers on. The horses see him and quickly realize this beast is not a threat; the creature, *Coryphodon,* is a harmless herbivore. So they let their guard down again and return to browsing quietly.

Meanwhile, another animal at the top of the mammalian predator list—one who lives well into the following epoch—moves about looking for his dinner. This is  the wolf-sized *Hyaenodon.* His skull is long with slender jaws.

His body is slim and he tends to walk on his toes rather than on flat feet. Using his sheer size, and strong jaws as his principal weapons, *Hyaenodon* can kill an Eocene horse with one bite. *Hyaenodon* hunts at night in small packs. They are a formidable enemy for all the smaller mammals in the jungle.

Lucky for horses, *Coryphodon* suddenly makes a menacing sound that resonates throughout the jungle, letting everyone know of his presence. Shaken by the loud noise, *Hyaenodon* slinks out of sight, as he is no match for the size and strength of *Coryphodon*.

This is an example of a symbiotic relationship between two herbivore species, *Coryphodon* and *Eohippus*. Through interspecies communication, the animals benefit one another's survival. This understanding and cooperative sharing, called mutualism in the field of biology, saves many animals from extinction.

Now fast forward to forty-eight million years B.C.E. By the middle Eocene, dozens of species of rodents and insect-eating mammals are thriving in the jungles of North America. Anteater-types are dining on armies of termites and flies, and many parasites afflict early horses. Except for an adaptation in their teeth, the mid-Eocene horses (*Orohippus, Mesohippus and Miohippus)* are similar to the earlier Eocene, Dawn Horse. Fortunately, these prehistoric horses adapt to their changing environment. By the end of the Eocene, more than twenty million years have passed; yet, the horse population is going strong.

Nevertheless, severe cold begins to create harsher weather conditions and many earlier species are lost. Despite this, primitive horses find a way to maintain their stability.

Oligocene Epoch: The Big Chill

The word Oligocene derives from the Greek for "few" and refers to "a time of few recent life forms." At the end of the Eocene and into the early Oligocene, a dramatic cooling trend takes place on the Earth. It is a time of biological chaos.

Horses begin to graze on grasses as well as browse on leaves and fruits, allowing them a greater variety of food to eat. During the Oligocene, the descendants of earlier horses become nearly fifty percent larger, but they are still much smaller than horses today. The senses of these horses are changing to reflect a shift in their habitat. Physically, they now have longer legs, allowing for freer movement and greater speed, and they stand about two feet tall. Their bigger skulls provide the greater lateral vision required for grazing safely in open grasslands. The Oligocene horse has also lost a toe, and stands predominantly on the middle toe, although the other two toes still provide traction when needed.

We can imagine a band of *Mesohippus* running to escape the devastating effects of an erupting volcano. Ashes and volcanic debris are scattered everywhere across the land, killing much of their food. The grasslands are inedible now. *Mesohippus* need to eat constantly. Because of their size, these horses cannot hibernate in winter like the smaller animals. *Mesohippus* often suffer from starvation due to the extreme fluctuations in climate and habitat.

This herd of *Mesohippus* is thin; some horses are close to death. Many have not eaten anything in days. They are struggling to protect themselves from predators who have been watching them from a distance. As we turn our attention to the horses, we can overhear a mare and her stallion talking about the survival of their young babies. The stallion says the killing power of the volcanic eruption depends upon how long it lasts. The mare wonders if it is possible to know whether the blasts will come again, and if so, how often.

As I wrote this section, I sensed that Buddy wanted to offer his own "memory pictures" about this ancient scene. When I asked him about it, he told the following story in the present tense. He said he would use the present tense, even though the scene is ancient. He said he wanted readers to immerse themselves in the story and experience it first-hand. Buddy was in the pasture with his mate Ellie while I tuned in telepathically to him from my office in the house.

We know the ground shakes before an event of this magnitude. There is even a distinct smell in the air. We usually do not wait to hear the eruption before we leave the area. But if the eruption is many miles away, we may not hear it coming. So we wait for our instincts to tell us what to do. The event you are observing in deep time happened many miles in the distance and the horses do not know it is coming.

When the wind catches hold of the debris and blows it over the land, the horses suffer. Their lungs inhale the soot and many have trouble breathing. This creates a greater dilemma for them. Should those of us who can run leave those of us who cannot behind? We know we cannot outrun the wind, though we wish in our hearts that we could. Therefore, we search for running water instead. The streams are not completely polluted with ash and if they are running we can drink. The stench is terrible. There are dead bodies everywhere. Death is all around us.

Ellie, Buddy's mate, now adds her perspective to the story, from an alpha mare's point of view.

I have a different perspective. I know the danger is in the air. So we must lower our intake of the air. I will put everyone into a mild trance that will limit the number of breaths we take. We will be like this during the day. Some will go down on their knees from the lack of fresh air. Others will survive. The mares are in charge of the herd from a survival perspective. So we will overcome this. I ask my herd to slow their breathing gradually. At night we roam and breathe normally. We keep our noses to the Earth. When the air clears, we will run. But for now we hide and stay low to the ground, and breathe.

Fortunately, the sky is filling with clouds and the air pressure is dropping. When it pours, the rain washes the leaves and the ground clean of ash, and the horses survive at least one more cycle of life.

At the end of the Oligocene, horses under-went a great evolutionary expansion. Several species in the two families *Mesohippus* and *Miohippus* expanded in the following epoch, the heyday of the horse.

Miocene Epoch: Heyday of the Horse

Fast forward to the Miocene, which begins about twenty-four million years B.C.E., and lasts approximately nineteen million years. The name Miocene is derived from the Greek words meion (meaning "less") and kainos (meaning "recent"), referring to the fact that fewer recent species were found in the rocks than those of more recent age.

It is a time of flourishing grass prairies and weeds as the thinning forests succumb to global cooling. The Earth is entering a deeper icehouse state. Until now, the ancient horses had dined on leaves, shrubs, herbs, fruit, berries, bark and roots. Now as the grasslands blow across the North American plains, the horses are adapting to a new diet. They are also learning how to share overlapping territories with other herds.

At the beginning of the Miocene, horses are less diverse compared with other epochs. Nevertheless, a pivotal group called *Parahippus* comes onto the scene. Scientists consider this group to be a transitional horse. *Parahippus* may be the evolutionary link between the more ancient forest-dwelling horses and the more recent plains-dwelling grazers. Their teeth are "high-crowned." High-crowned teeth permit horses to eat grasses because high-crowned teeth continue to grow as the abrasive grass wears them down.

As the grasslands spread and the forests recede, horses continue to graze and browse, much the same as they do today. When the grass is depleted, modern horses eat leaves, shrubs, and tree bark much like their ancient ancestors.

Enured to the Land: Buddy on the Miocene Epoch

Since Buddy has a lot to offer on this subject, let us hear his views again about Ancestor Horse in his heyday.

The hard ground gives way to our speed and we know our longer legs can take advantage of the Earth in this way. The Earth rumbles and ruptures and the birds tremble. The birds escape the explosions into the sky. Then, the sky pours out its life on us. The drinking water is good. Imagine pure oxygen, pure water, pure land, and pure fire. We eat less when we travel. The whole Earth is our oyster. We travel in herds of thousands.

We see many different kinds of horses from many different places. Predator animals track us for days at a time. The most joyful thing in life for us is the idea that horses have no boundaries. This is a time of freedom, and running, and communing with other creatures

like us, and listening to the winds of change and knowing when it is
time to move on.

Paradise Lost

At the end of the Miocene, about five million years, B.C.E.,
horse diversity in North America diminishes to three groups.
In the tropical climates only three to five species remain. This
is also about the time that horses begin locking their knees.
Combined with other amazing changes, such as longer legs and
reduced side toes, these adaptations allow horses to survive in
other parts of the world. Horses now travel many more miles
per day than before and can take advantage of different foods
during less-plentiful seasons.

By the end of the Miocene, the great horse radiation is
unfortunately wiped out. Competition with neighboring cud-
chewing hoofed herbivores, such as deer and bison, has
affected the horse populations. Unlike ruminants that have four
stomachs, horses have only one. Horses now have to spend
more than half their waking hours eating and this renders the
end of the heyday of the horse.

Water is scarce because it is frozen and sea levels are
dropping. Though the number of horses is diminishing, the
number of horse species remains the same. The genus Equus
successfully maintains its diversity with thirty species.

During the Pleistocene, the next epoch, which lasts
from 1.8 million to 10,000 years ago, horses are roaming in
North and South America, Eurasia, and Africa. But at the end
of the last Inter-glacial Age, mammoths, mastodons, and
horses all face extinction.

The Earth cools during the Oligocene, through the

Miocene, and into the Pliocene. The Miocene boundaries are not set by easily identifiable worldwide events, but at regional boundaries between the warmer Oligocene and the cooler Pliocene. The plants and animals of the Miocene are modern looking. Birds are well established and even whales and seals are thriving.

By the end of the Pleistocene, some 10,000 years ago, *Homo sapiens* begin killing off whole herds of reindeer, musk ox, and woolly mammoth. Fortunately for these animals, they can run away from humans. Yet, when animals start to compete with one another for food, as the forests and savannas become treeless tundra, those animals who do not adapt to life on the tundra either die or move south. Equus moves to South America during the Ice Age and manages to replace the native species there called *Hippidions*. Equus reaches the Straits of Magellan, but unlike North American horses, the South American *Equidae* live until a few thousand years ago. By the time the Spaniards arrive, these horses mysteriously die out too. Though horses become extinct in the Americas, Equus continues in the Old World — on the steppes of central Asia, and in Africa, where they give rise to the modern zebra.

Horses' Recent Ancestors

 Horses do not reestablish themselves in America until 1493 when Columbus and his men transport domesticated European breeds in ships during their second voyage. Horses that travel in ships are suspended in slings (with their feet off the floor.) The seamen think this will protect the animals from rough seas. But as

anyone who knows horses might suspect, this is a fatal mistake.

Scientists recognize three types of primitive, wild horses as the foundation for today's modern horse. The Asian Wild Horse, *E. caballus przewalski*, or Przewalski's Horse, is the only wild horse still surviving in captivity. The other two, the Forest Horse of Poland and the last surviving wild Tarpan, went extinct during the 18th century. These horses are common in Europe during the last Ice Age and are the horses that the artist-hunting Cro-Magnons depicted on cave walls during the Upper Paleolithic in France and Spain about 17,000 years ago.

CHAPTER THREE

The Shamanic Connection: The Role of the Horse in Ancient Culture

"Ayla had known how to speak once, and, though the language was not the same, she had learned the feel, the rhythm, the sense of spoken language. She had forgotten how to speak verbally because her survival depended upon another mode of communication, and because she wanted to forget the tragedy that had left her alone."

Valley of the Horses

~ Jean M. Auel

The Old Stone Age, or An Evening with the Magnons

The Paleolithic or "Old Stone" age is an era set apart by the development of the first stone tools. It extended from the introduction of flint tools, more or less 2.5 million years ago, to the introduction of agriculture and the end of the Pleistocene epoch around 10,000 BC. During the Paleolithic, early humans banded together in small groups; they lived on plants and the wild animals they could kill or scavenge.

Although the Paleolithic age was characterized by stone cutting tools, the early humans we have named Cro -Magnon, were also using wood and bone as implements. They also adopted other organic materials for tools, such as leather and vegetable fibers, but these have not been preserved to any great degree.

Humans gradually evolved from these early members of the genus *Homo*, such as *Homo habilis*, who used tools, into modern humans, *Homo sapiens sapiens*, during the last Ice Age. At the end of this era, specifically during the Upper Paleolithic, clan members started to produce their earliest works of art and engaged in ritual burials and ceremonial hunting ceremonies.

An evening with the extended family of a Cro Magnon clan might have looked something like this:

Twenty members of a single tribe gather outside the entrance to a local cave that has been their main gathering hall for many seasons. It is dusk on a warm summer evening in the southern part of the country we now call France.

Several girls, dressed in deerskin thongs, are playing stickball with their puppy-sized wolf dogs. It is the time in prehistory when humankind is experimenting with training the European Grey Wolf to help them with hunting.

The older members of the tribe are preparing a feast for later this evening at the mouth of the cave. Everyone will eat after the ceremonies are over. Smoke rises into the star-studded sky with a bright, orange harvest moon waxing overhead. The smell of rabbit roasting in a sauce of blueberries and sweet potatoes fills the air. The repetitive drone of distant drumming reminds the clan of a neighboring tribe, not far in the distance.

A large breasted woman, dressed in feathers and fur, begins to play a simple melody on a smooth flute, sculpted from the hollow bone of a cave bear's leg. The others begin chanting and dancing in rhythmic motion.

When everyone arrives, they go deeper into the cave for the evening's events. It is a long-awaited ritual, filled with music and drumming. Everyone feels the excitement.

Once inside, they sit on bear skin throw rugs large enough to accommodate an entire family. Flickering firelight dances on the cave walls, creating moving images. The old Shaman, covered in a woolly mammoth hide, begins recounting his ancestral legends as the clan taps on deerskin drums. Sharing meat and remembering the ancestors, these cave dwellers strongly resemble a modern-day family.

Several wolf dogs huddle together at the mouth of the cave to devour the remains of a kill, which they helped to bring down. The dogs have a special relationship with their cave dwelling friends. Not as tame as their descendants today, the primitive wolf dogs protect human property from predatory carnivores; in return they are given food and shelter.

As wild dogs become more domesticated, they are permitted to help hunt for wild horses. The wild horses provide raw materials for the tribe's tools and other daily necessities. The horse's stomach makes a useful bag for carrying water or fat. Since there is less rainfall during the Ice Age, water is scarce in certain areas, making carrying water in a bladder-like container essential.

The skin of the horse provides leather for boots, jackets, coats, and tents. Cut into strips, horsehide can be used for tying and carrying equipment. The tail and mane of the horse have strong fibers, which, when twisted, are made into thread for sewing or stringing beads and pendants. The twisting of the threads makes for a strong rope.

Horses' bones are also useful. Hunters sculpt them into needles, awls, and spear tips. They extract fat and grease from the horse and use it to waterproof their clothing. The grease is good for smearing onto the skin for insulation against the cold, or as protection from insect bites in summer. Horse fat is smokeless, and an excellent source of light for dark caves.

These prehistoric caves may have played an important role in the hunting and spiritual practices of early people. The informal name of Cro-Magnon was used to refer to those living with the Neanderthals at the end of the last Ice Age (ca. 35,000-10,000 years ago). They were given the name because in France in 1868, several skeletons were found in a rock shelter of the same name.

Caves: Facebook® of the Stone Age

The oldest known symbols used for human communication were created some 20,000 years ago by our ancestors. Just as small children learn how to draw before they master verbal communication, so did our ancestors first attempt to record and communicate using cave paintings. One of the oldest examples of cave art is 30,000 years old, called Chauvet Cave, in Southern France. Three explorers were surveying another cave nearby when they discovered a huge network of galleries and interior rooms over 400 meters long.

Many speculate that ancient caves were initiation sites for rites of passage for different clans. The cave could have been symbolic of an initiate's transition into other realms during a ritual ceremony, and it may have represented the descent into the underworld. Prehistoric caves may have also played an important part in the initiation of North American Shamans, as it was in caves that Shamans had their spiritual visions and dreams.

The animal drawings in some caves could have additional meaning because of their placement. The artists used natural rock formations or stalagmite deposits for the placement of their images. This suggests that the cave itself was thought to embody the mystical animal's influence already, and that the animals' souls may have existed in these places primordially. As the Ice Age ended, Cro-Magnons moved north, completely disappearing from Europe all together.

Shamanism

Shamanism is an ancient method of psycho spiritual medicine, originating more than 25,000 years ago with the hunting cultures of Siberia and Central Asia. The English word Shaman is derived from the Siberian Tungus word *saman*, meaning "technique of ecstasy." A Shaman is the master of trance and ecstasy. He or she is the spiritual leader for the tribe who possesses the powers the community needs for healing illness and imbalance.

The basis of the Shaman's work is grounded in the Shaman's mastery of the technique of ecstasy, in which the

Shaman enters an altered state of consciousness, known as the trance state. During this experience, the Shaman's soul leaves his body and travels to nonordinary reality to speak with the spirits for help with healing. The Shaman is the mediator between the clan and the spirit world. A Shaman's intervention can promote successful hunting and food production. He/she is charged with keeping the tribe's equilibrium.

Traditional Shamanic rituals include singing, dancing, chanting, drumming, and storytelling. As a specialist who can see and cure diseases of the human soul, a Shaman must know how to work with the spirits, rather than being possessed by them. The Shaman communicates with the patient's demons while invoking the help of the nature spirits. The Shaman works with those in the community whose souls have abandoned their bodies, even when the individual is alive. If the soul of the person has strayed to distant realms, it can fall prey to demons and sorcerers. Thus, the Shaman diagnoses the problem and searches for the wandering soul. Once the Shaman finds it he helps the patient's soul return safely to the person's body.

Shamans believe there are many worlds beyond this Earthly dimension, and that all creation is alive--rocks, plants, animals, trees, birds and fish. The Shaman knows and communicates with all of these forces of nature for healing.

The Horse in Shamanic Cultures

Mircea Eliade writes in his book, *Shamanism: Archaic Techniques of Ecstasy,* that some Mongol Shamans see the "white horse of the Shamans" as the preeminent Shamanic animal. The horse's gallop and dizzying speed are the traditional expressions of Shamanic flight and reminiscent of ecstasy. To a Mongolian Shaman, the horse is a dual being---the warrior's steed as well as a guide for the soul. The horse is the spirit mount of the Shaman. The Shaman rides his spirit horse during the celestial journey, and it is the horse that carries the souls of the dead into other worlds.

Alongside the horse's historic role as a war machine, horses have been seen as invaluable fellow travelers, connected with all life. In Hinduism, the horse is associated with Vishnu's final appearance on Earth, during which time he brings peace and redemption.

Heartbeats, Hoof Beats, Drumbeats

The Shaman says the "drum is our horse." The beating drum becomes the horse. At a fundamental level, the sound of horses' hooves echo our own heartbeats and the pulse of life itself. Even before birth, we are imprinted in our mother's womb with her, and our own, rhythmic heartbeat. Clip clop, clip clop, whether real or symbolic, it is a sound with which we are familiar. For the older child, the rocking horse and merry-go-round also replicate the rhythmic rocking of prenatal life.

The drum becomes a vehicle that transports the Shaman on a journey into unknown realms. To reach the heavens and experience ecstasy, the Shaman employs the drum and the horse to "come out of himself," and to make the mystical journey possible. Metaphorically, the horse enables a Shaman to fly through the air and reach the heavens.[2]

According to most primitive cultures, the tribal Shaman receives his initiation in a cave adorned with the

---

[2] Mircea Eliade, *Shamanism: Archaic Techniques of Ecstacy.*

drawings of animals he would teach others to honor and ultimately kill for food and clothing. Some believe the Shaman and early hunting tribesmen used their intuitive abilities to communicate with each other, through art, dance, and music. And through their intuition, coupled with strong instincts, our ancestors learned how to communicate with animals, both in their care, and those they killed for food and clothing.

Although hunting magic in ancient caves is an unproven theory, some important spiritual motivations, including Shamanism, could have inspired the hunters' cave art. Many prehistorians believe that the cave art, in which horses played a dominant part, was divinely inspired and often created by the Shaman/healer/priest/magician/ of the clan.

Animism

Indigenous cultures practicing Shamanism today commonly have an animistic view of the world. The word animism is derived from the Latin *anima*, which means "breath of life." Animists believe that all of life—animals, plants, fish, birds, trees, people, even rocks and rivers—share the same "breath of life." Accordingly, animists strive to live in harmony with all living things.

In animism, there is no ladder of supremacy or hierarchy between species. Rather, the view is that souls or spirits live not only in humans and animals but also in all natural phenomena—thunder, lightning, meteor showers. Animists attribute souls to abstract ideas, such as the ideas embodied in words or metaphors in mythology. They also believe the souls of animals can be embodied in the cave paintings. The Paleolithic drawings of horses may not have been simple artistic renderings of real animals, but rather the 'spirit animals' of the day.

In the world of the animist, communication is vital between all species and spiritual beings. Prayers and offerings are made to the spirits to ensure the goodwill of the spirits. Many indigenous cultures give gifts to please the tree spirits so that the trees may thrive. When choosing a tree for carving a ceremonial mask or drum, they simply do not cut the tree down. They explain to the spirit of the tree how the wood will be used, and they ask permission for the sacrifice. If the wood is made into a drum, the musician speaks to the spirit of the instrument as he begins to play, thereby establishing a co-creative relationship between him and the spirit of the drum.

Animists believe that it is wasteful to exploit anything in nature that sacrifices its life. North American Indians once used all the parts of the buffalo they killed for fuel, food, clothing, and shelter. Nothing of the animal was carelessly wasted. To waste a life was dishonorable.

The basis for ancient human beliefs can only be a matter of speculation because there is so little concrete evidence. However, we may rely on insight to inform us that ancient societies did not consciously choose to become religious–that the split between the sacred and the secular is more recent.

In the past, there most likely was no division between peoples' spiritual beliefs and the rest of life. This is different from how we delineate our religious, professional, and social lives today. In ancient times, spirituality was likely mixed with everything else. It was blended with the environment, techniques for finding food, procreation, and harmonizing with the elements.

If we reviewed all of the religions of the world, we would find a mind-boggling variety. Yet, upon deeper discovery, we might also find that human worship, or the quest for the spiritual, has three objects or objectives — nature, humans themselves, and that of an absolute reality, neither human nor of nature, but which is in them, and at the same time beyond or above them.

Many believe that humans began spiritual worship by revering nature. However, when we began to exploit nature we were also left with a spiritual void. Subsequently, humans were compelled to fill the void, but were confronted with answering the question of whether to substitute the worship of nature for the worship of themselves, or of a higher power.

In the 21st century, in which human societies are being linked into a single global community within the framework of worldwide technology, the complexity of ideas about worship continues to underlie many of our current world controversies. Shall we worship ourselves? Shall we worship God? Shall we worship nature? Of these three, which have been competing for our devotion for a long time, the worship of nature is by far the oldest, and the most deeply rooted in our collective psyche.

Whatever the original religion of humans was is not known. The worship of God, which has been brought into our minds by present-day religion, is a revival, not an innovation of the earliest religion of humans. It is conceivable that we continued to worship nature until we began to manipulate nature for our own purposes, causing a split between the Earth, the animals and us.

Despite the apparent victory of our conquering nature, the Earth and the animals, reverence for all life is still deeply embedded in our religions. We see evidence of this in Hinduism, Christianity, and Islam, and these elements of nature-worship are more than just the die-hard remains of dead religions. They suggest that below the surface of the human psyche, the worship of nature is still alive and well. It is alive because nonhuman nature, over which we think we won victory in the Upper Paleolithic, is just one half of the nature. The more formidable half, with which we still need to cope, is the wild nature we find within ourselves.

New insights into the vast underground temples of nature worship have shown this type of worship—long since argued from the rational surface of life—has maintained itself at the lower levels of human consciousness. Why? Because, at these depths, human nature is still just as wild as it ever was. The intellect may have gained victory over physical nature, but we are just beginning to explore the nature of the still untamed inner psyche/nature.[3]

In any event, you are probably curious to know what part the horse plays in a discussion about the origin of religion. The overwhelming dominance of the horse in the mind of Upper Paleolithic humans, and the tremendous cultural importance placed on horses, as seen in the careful placement of their bones and teeth in hearths and later in Neolithic burial sites, suggests that the horse was a sacred animal. Ancient humans also practiced magic rituals in which the horse played an integral role.[4]

Totemism

In *Webster's New World College Dictionary, Fourth Edition* the word totem is defined as an entity that watches over a group of people, family, clan, or tribe. In more recent

---

[3] Arnold Toynbee, *A Historical Approach to Religion*.

[4] Mircea Eliade, *Shamanism: Archaic Techniques of Ecstacy.*

times, totems are said to also support individuals. If the ancestor of a human clan is nonhuman, it is called a totem. Normally these beliefs have an accompanying totemic myth attached to them.

Although the term totem is of Ojibwe origin in North America, totemic beliefs are not limited to Native Americans. Similar beliefs are present throughout much of the world, including Africa, Asia, Australia, Eastern Europe, Western Europe, and the Arctic polar region.

Animal totems are embedded in Paleolithic cave art as well. The totem mirrors a person's former incarnation prior to his or her present physical form and his or her basic nature. The idea of a totem is the primordial realization of the duality of life–a celebration of life in the moment, as well as recognizing the ancestors and their traditions.

We become our true selves when we detach from our shadows and focus in the present moment. The totem acts as a way back to our preconscious existence. We are linked to our beginnings through totemic rituals, both as spiritual beings and as manifestations of nature in the form of a totem.

Each person is closely tied to his or her preexistent archetypal form, whether flora, fauna, or some other natural phenomenon such as water or wind. When in the moment, a person cannot disavow his or her totem because it represents his archetypal form. To do so would be to deny what he was at the time of his own creation.

Understanding the idea of totemic identity enables us to begin a dialogue with domestic and wild animals. When we call upon our totem animal, we can receive help in exploring animal communication. Our totem animals help us to perceive the thoughts, feelings, and emotional states of both companion and wild animals through mental telepathy.

It is likely that as early humans we took the young animal of a killed adult back to our campsite after a hunt, and ended up raising it. Since playing with cute baby animals gives so much pleasure and reward, an unusual interspecies relationship between humans and animals began to take shape.

Prehistoric humans may also have kept horses in captivity for food during the winter months. But finding them friendly, and not so hard to care for, needing only a modest plot of grass and water each day, we became enamored with them. As time passed, nomads learned that the strength of horses, with their four legs, was better than their own. It is possible that a group of humans, who had the horse as their totem animal, were the first people to experiment with harnessing the power of the horse. This may have been the beginning of the domestication process for horses as a species.

The Spiritual Wisdom of Our Ancestors

Many indigenous peoples' cosmologies are based on a spiritual relationship with animals and the Earth. Yet, reverence for the holy caves of the Earth, in the form of spiritual temples, has diminished in modern life. Even so, our first spiritual practices originated from a direct relationship with the natural world and animals, both real and imagined.

Indigenous spiritual wisdom addresses communion with the Earth, and the protection of the seeds of life, without separating humanity from the whole of nature. It is understood and believed in Native American cosmology that failing to honor the laws of nature can reap severe consequences.

We need to learn how to revere the holy temples of the Earth once again, nature's womb, and the sacred caves. We need to remember how to honor the laws of nature. We need to renew our kinship with the source of our creation, the source of our privilege to live on the Earth, with all her wonderful creatures, in peace and harmony.

Humans and horses once enjoyed a long prehistoric relationship that originated thousands of years ago when we shared a psychic, spiritually-based nonverbal system of communication. This is evidenced in the cave paintings. Paradoxically, as we attempt to move toward interplanetary communication, we would be wise to remember that within the heart of ancient interspecies relationships lies a "jewel within a stone," awaiting our rediscovery. That jewel (telepathy between species) is the essential healing bond that animals and humans shared. Within this bond is a gift that can guide us on our spiritual and interplanetary quest. In addition, since humans have denied the essential core of this telepathic connection for so long, it is important that we renew it, or at least reinvent it, so that we may evolve cooperatively and embrace our commonality with other species on Earth.

When early people began to settle down and build permanent dwellings, they also began to subvert the heart of this wonderful association with the wild beasts. We learned almost everything we know about nature from plants and animals and we are still learning. We once needed animals to show us how to survive severe weather and how to find food, water, and shelter. Today, animals are again showing humans how to live communally on the Earth.

About the same time we began to justify exploiting not only animals, but also other human beings, nations, races, and sexes, we started to lose our psychic ties with nature. Armed with this reasoning a person had only to demonstrate the "other" was not fully human or "closer to an animal" to establish right of dominion.

According to Aristotle, women were also deficient in a rational soul, and the relationship of male to female was naturally that of the superior with the inferior. Many humans still feel above and apart from the "others" in nature, and that we have "dominion over the Earth." This paradigm, which is slowly drawing down, dominates our worldview and has shaped modern societies across all boundaries of nation, race and religion.

The new paradigm focuses on a more holistic worldview — seeing the world as an integrated whole that functions as an interconnected network. Now, more than ever, we are recognizing our fundamental interdependence upon each other as we share the same ecological concerns.

There is a shift for humans to live more sustainable lives and become more aware of our collective carbon footprint. We are realizing, by embracing our relationships with nonhumans that we are truly in partnership with everything alive.

If we understand the idea of the inherent ability we share to communicate with nature, we can begin a dialogue with the deeper "wild" nature within ourselves and renew the awe that this presence inspires. We can cease denying the power within us. Nature's absolute power over us, and within us, is awe inspiring--even when we choose to harness it.

Somehow the primordial "wildness" inside of us remains bound, like a prisoner in the cave of the psyche awaiting the moment to break free. By recognizing all life is ongoing and never-ending, we realize our part in the act of creation lies in the present moment.

According to Jeremy Schmidt in his book, *The Spirit of Mother Earth*, "The Iroquois have a principle: Consider the impact of every decision as far ahead as the seventh generation." Imagine the changes if the Industrial Revolution had been considered with that principle in mind. No conscious person would have ever subjected seven generations to the greatest amount of chemicals to be deposited into the air, land, rivers, and seas in modern history. Human communication with nature is Earth's original green movement.

The truth is that we inherited our ancestors' innate ability to communicate with nonhuman nature. The ability is inborn, as much as the inborn ability to hunt and gather food, to love our families, and teach our children. We need to remember this, as it is at the heart of who we are.

Long ago, the Earth spoke to our ancestors. What they learned was that we are not separate from the Earth. Each is a part of the other, and all parts are sacred. The land is full of power. The rivers swarm with fish. The plains are trodden by the hooves of deer, elk, buffalo, and horses. Plants grow according to seasons, sun, rain, and wind. We watch the moon to record its signs. The Mohawks say, "Our grandparents of old, they were saying. Listen to her, all, to the Earth our Mother, to what she is saying. People, listen all."

Humans are aware of life's most basic rules. All motions are circular. No action is free of consequence. All life begins from the ground beneath our feet. We are related to all things in flesh and spirit. In addition, for us, solace comes from being aligned with the natural rhythms and forces of the Earth. We cannot conquer, overcome, or bend the rules without suffering the results for ourselves and our descendants.

These lessons of nature, once denied by science and philosophy as superstition, are more relevant in today's ecological movement. At a time when the kinship between people and the Earth has reached an all-important crossroads, the ancient knowledge of Shamanism, animism, and totemism, the "knowings" of the indigenous peoples and animals, are being revisited, not as superstitious nonsense, but as the wisdom of the ages, past, present and future.

CHAPTER FOUR

Into the Forest of Transformation: The Spiritual Emergence of the Horse

"One way or another, we all have to find what best fosters the flowering of our humanity in this contemporary life, and dedicate ourselves to that."

~ Joseph Campbell

The late Joseph Campbell once told a story about a hunter in Celtic mythology who became enthralled by the timeless beauty of a white stag. Following it deeper and deeper into the forest, he realized that he was in a totally new place, and that the stag had simply disappeared. The story illustrates Campbell's popular saying: "Follow Your Bliss." It also highlights the abruptness that transformation can bring into our lives.

When I followed my bliss, I came to a completely new place in my writing with Buddy. Instead of continuing the book in chronological fashion, I found myself learning a completely new language, with new skills that expanded my spiritual vocabulary into the world of Shamanic mythology: The myths and stories of Shamans who journey to heal the Earth and her creatures. Buddy reshaped my relationship with almost everything--family, partners, friends, and my creative work with him.

What I did not know, however, was whether Campbell, or Buddy, had ever spoken of the amount of life-changing events that following your bliss can create, and that the integration of these new experiences can take years to achieve.

Sparing you, the reader, the time it took me and confusion it caused me when I began to integrate these new experiences, (which continues) I will simply take you to the edge of the 'Forest of Transformation' and let you go with these simple words, "Wings of flight open for those who have the courage to fly!"

The Spiritual Messages of Ancestor Horse

"In that time before there was Time, there was Grandfather Fire. Around Grandfather Fire sat the Circle of Animal Brothers, who, speaking in that Sacred Language of Spirit, told their Tellings. Through these Tellings, Grandfather Fire gave rise to creation"
~ Jade Wah-oo Grigorio

So begins the mythic telling of Shamanic Creation when the Two-Leggeds were one of the Animal Brothers in the place of our Origin.

Grigorio further comments, "The Two-Leggeds left the Circle of our Animal Brothers, left the embrace of Grandfather Fire, and went into the Darkness, into the land of Death, the land we refer to as Life. In this place of Death, we lost our ability to communicate in the Sacred Language of Spirit."

For the past fifteen years, Buddy, Ellie and I have been on the path to help the world regain this lost ability to communicate in the Sacred Language of Spirit. I first looked at how humans lost the ability, and then asked why it has remained lost to us. During my "due diligence," this is what I found.

Thomas Berry, author of *The Universe Story*, writes that the end of the Cenozoic Era may be caused by humans' inability to be 'present' to the Earth. The Cenozoic era is the most recent of the three classic geological eras and covers the period from 65.5 million years ago to the present. Berry, writes that Westerners have been in a daze about their spiritual relationship with the Earth ever since the first great philosopher of the modern era, René Descartes, the father of modern philosophy in 17th century Europe.

Descartes was a French mathematician, scientist, and writer who pursued mathematical and scientific truths that led him to reject common scholastic traditions. He was more concerned about advancing human knowledge through the natural sciences. However, he feared condemnation from his colleagues and was careful how he expressed his radical views. He believed that two kinds of substances existed in the universe — mental substance and corporeal substance. Humans, he said, were composed of mind (which he equated with the soul) and body. Nonhuman animals, however, were mindless automata--machines. The traditional interpretation was that animals had no feelings. Nonhuman animals had conscious feelings, but not self-conscious awareness of those feelings.

Animals could feel, but could make no sense of their feelings; they could not associate their feelings with the outside world. Descartes denied that animals had minds. Animals also had no self-consciousness. Animals only "felt joy" and other physical emotions. In response to physical stimuli, they would respond mechanically by dancing about, appearing happy, although these "animal machines" could not consciously feel anything akin to happiness.

Thus, Descartes declared that animals do not feel "pain in the strictest sense," since they lack understanding or mind. Animals are not aware. These views did not go unchallenged, even in Descartes' time. Voltaire (1694-1778) famously wrote a generation later, "Answer me, Machinist, has nature arranged all the means of feeling in the animal, so that it may not feel?"

Before the 17th century, humans viewed the world as having an anima, a soul. Every being was ennobled with a voice that could speak about divine mysteries. Nature was the Muse of poets, musicians, philosophers, and mystics. But according to Descartes, if the natural world was a mere mechanism, there could be no sharing of life with the birds or animals or plants because these unthinking mechanisms did not have souls. Consequently, people reduced these things to nothing more than economic value. As this idea took root in the Age of Reason, it created a long and destructive anthropocentric period in European history that persists today in modern thought.

In the 20th century, Thomas Berry (born in 1914) wanted a new model of mutual presence between humans, nature, plants, and animals. In his book, *The Dream of the Earth*, he notes, "If we do not get it straight now, we cannot expect a significant remedy for the present distress we are experiencing. Because of our short sightedness, my generation never heard the voices of that vast multitude of inhabitants of the planet. We had no communion with the nonhuman world. We would go to the seashore or mountains for recreation and realize only a moment of aesthetic joy. Our ideas were too superficial to establish reverence or intimate rapport with nature. We showed no sensitivity to the powers of the various phenomena in the natural world, no awe restrained our assault on nature to extract human advantage, even if it meant tearing the entire fabric of the planet apart. So, the information we could have gathered from these other children of God, the plants and animals, was lost to us."

Animals and Nature: Lost and Found

Is the ability to communicate with nature truly lost, or can we still reconnect and remember? If we can refocus our spiritual relationship with nature and let it teach us, this awakened state of kinship may be what we need to realign ourselves with planet Earth.

Today, corporations are adopting the time-honored philosophy of present moment awareness into their stress management programs, with the belief that learning to live more mindfully brings contentment, and more productivity. But many people are too busy and allow life to slip away.

We are scattering ourselves by doing things we think we should be doing, instead of doing what we know is truly meaningful. We are so preoccupied with deadlines that we miss important moments in our lives. We are so out of touch with the myths and rhythms of life that we allow gross imbalances to occur. And, we are passing these legacies down to our children.

We are killing wild species at a prodigious rate, species that have priceless knowledge and experience to share, experiences that can guide us toward global and spiritual sustainability. In an era of fast food, computers, and technology, we are carelessly diminishing our experience of nature. We actually fear wild animals, their habitats, and their knowledge.

Young adults do not know where to begin with this legacy. They do not know where they belong in the scheme of things because the myths of the past do not support life as we know it today. The old myths, the ones that held us together long ago, and made us whole as a species, do not spur us toward spiritual growth presently. We have distanced ourselves from the light in our own hearts, our dreams and visions. We have lost sight of our spiritual roots. We are advancing technologically, but spiritually, we are still like little children—lost, afraid, and wandering unattended.

So, how can we make the shift? It takes faith to step into the void to find our way back home. Yet, if we tell new myths in new ways, these myths will help us to discover our common ground with nature. Humans can benefit from new myths that point to our collective core beliefs in the circle of life. The animals can help us to remember who we are, and how we came into being. New myths can help us to understand ourselves holistically as they shed light on our potential together.

The Indigenous Connection: Equus in Dreamtime

In order to understand the spirit of the horse and their creation myths, we will look at the example of the Indigenous connection to the Dreamtime. Indigenous people all over the world have stressed the importance of creation myths. Australian Aborigines have clear views of these sacred narratives. To these people, every meaningful activity of life on Earth leaves behind a vibrational signature, the same as a plant leaves its image in a seed.

The shape of the land--the mountains, rocks, rivers--along with their unseen vibrations, echo the events that brought those places to life. In short, the uncorrupted world is a symbolic imprint of the metaphysical beings whose actions created the world.

Just as a seed, the potential of a place or thing is joined to the memory of its origins. The Aborigines call this potentiality "The Dreaming." In Dreamtime the holiness of the Earth is affirmed. In extraordinary states of awareness, what Shamans call nonordinary reality, humans are conscious and attuned to the intrinsic Dreamings of the Earth.

Animals also have the capacity and the power to expand their minds into extraordinary states of consciousness. My horses have often shown their otherworldly journeys into The Dreamtime to me. They spoke about how they intuit The Dreamings of the Earth for their own species. Buddy once told me that he can "feel" the hoof beats of his species running all over the Earth.

Horses are able to expand their awareness naturally because their survival depends on it. They must be physically and emotionally in cycle with the seasons---sun, stars, moon, and all parts of the environment.

The Dreamtime is 'the time before time,' and that time is the time of the creation of all things. They refer to creation time as The Dreaming. The Dreaming parallels an individual's or a group's core beliefs or spirituality. Indigenous Australians have what they call Kangaroo Dreaming and Shark Dreaming, Honey Ant Dreaming, or a combination of Dreamings that relate to their land and nature.

Aborigines believe their Ancestor Spirits came to the Earth in human and other forms. It is how the land, plants, and animals received their forms, as we know them. Then, the

Spirits established kinship with the humans and nonhumans, and wherever they traveled and stopped to rest they created rivers, mountains, and oceans.

Aboriginal sacred stories affirm the spiritual creation of these sacred places. When the Ancestor Spirits completed their work, they shifted back into the animals' bodies, stars, hills, or other objects. For the Aborigines, the past is alive and vital. The ancestral powers have not departed. They are present in the forms into which they changed at the end of The Dreamtime.

Aboriginal stories show these ideas in their myths and stories. Mythmaking is a lifelong part of their culture. Storytelling plays a critical role. They use storytelling to educate their children and help their children understand how they came into being---how the land became inhabited. These stories show how their tribes must behave and where to find food. Thus, the storytellers pass on their creation myths throughout the ages; this is how creation myths are integrated into their peoples' Dreaming.

An Aboriginal medicine man speaks about the bush and the differences between his ways and those of the white man. For the white man, the bush is something from which to garner profit. For the Aborigine, the bush is that part of him that relates to nature.

"When you go out into the bush, all the beings, they see you coming. I suppose they say to themselves, 'Oh no, not another one of those again.' Because the bush, every part of the bush, has had some sort of confrontation with humans. Most of it's been bad. A lot of the bush is untouched, left untouched, but all the spiritual beings know about humans and their destructive spirit. They are still reaching out to us, whether we realize it or not. They are reaching out because we have the power of life and death over them. They are reaching out to us for peace."

"There are a lot of things the aboriginal medicine men like---we sit on top of great hills, or a big mountain. We do not have great mountains. Our hills are about two or three thousand feet and that's it. But to us it affords the energy, the luxury to sit on top of a hill crossing our legs, closing our eyes, getting in contact with nature. To let nature come to us because nature has been waiting for us to come, all the time. As we sit on the hill, nature is just reaching out and we feel the breeze coming and we feel nature talking to us. We start to communicate with nature by opening our ears, opening ourselves. We open our inner selves, we start to breathe fresh air, we let everything else out. Once we let everything else out it will let everything else in through our ears. We concentrate and make communication with nature. As we do, it leads us to other things, like spiritual travel. You must be at ease for spiritual travel. As we do these sorts of things, we become aware of what's there. Then we have that feeling of being at one with nature."

The Power of Myth

Joseph Campbell wrote in *The Power of Myth* that "myths refer to complex stories, songs, rituals, dances, rites of passage, and cultural customs created to inform and instruct individuals, families, tribes, communities, cultures, and the entire world in which we live. If we look deeper at our myths, we will discover our ancestral roots." According to Campbell, most of the world's populations are unenlightened about the myths that influence their lives today.

Because myths exist on both personal and cultural

levels, we have myths for both individuals and groups. Personal myths consist of collected beliefs, stories, and dreams that inform a single person about how to behave and think. Cultural myths are all the personal myths distilled in a consensual reality, creating a general agreement between individuals in a group. Cultural myths often govern social rules, values, ethics, and behavior. Together, personal and cultural myths deeply influence our collective psyche—worldview, sense of place, and sense of belonging.

Most myths are passed down through families, both living and deceased, by religious and cultural groups, or anyone who can travel the depths of the unconscious, and return to tell the story. Elaborating on the power of myth, Campbell notes:

"Myths contain clues for those who wish to plumb the depths of their spiritual potentialities. They point to the hidden opening through which boundless cosmic energies come into our awareness and self expression." The mythic imagination is the voice of the psyche that connects the knowing mind with the unconscious and the archetypal mythic realm---the Shaman's world.

This connecting force of myth heightens communication between the spiritual and the mundane. It bridges spiritual abilities which flow into our conscious awareness. The force aids communication between human and nonhuman species. Some believe if it were not for the mythic imagination, neither intellectual transformation nor evolution of consciousness would take place. Since Shamanism grounds itself in a kinship with the mythic realm and the imagination, some believe it has played an important role in the process of evolution.

Campbell compared a living myth with an iceberg,

where ten percent of the myth is visible above the horizon of consciousness, and ninety percent lies beneath the surface, in the unconscious. The submerged iceberg and the area of the unconscious are where we find the mythic realm.

I wondered whether mythology acts as a container for animals' psyches in the same way it does for people, and whether animal myths are passed down from one generation to the next in the same way human myths are handed down. The idea struck me that animals' spiritual relatives are alive and circulating among them and that their energy impacts their modern descendants in the same way it impacts human descendants.

After finishing the chapter about Ancestor Horse, I asked Buddy about creation myths for horses. From then, instead of the scientific account I had written about ancient horses, I explored the idea of creation mythology. I asked Buddy to tell his own personal creation myth and creation myths for the species Equus.

I was in awe at the possibility of using my Shamanic training and telepathic ability to communicate with Buddy to discover his creation myths and the collective myths for his species. Since all cultures, no matter what species, have stories to tell about their origins, why not horses? Most myths have been, until now, anthropocentric, using animals as symbols to enhance the telling of human mythology.

Once I realized I could work with animals to tell their myths, I contemplated whether animals also had the same universal symbolism that indigenous people have to tell myths. So I asked Ellie, Buddy's mate, to comment on the use of symbolism in animal mythology.

You can know a symbol without words, because a symbol points to the un-nameable and the unknowable. Symbols are the psyche's way of journeying through the deeper mysteries and initiations of life. Symbols are a focal point, used to distract us away from our inner impurities and allow purer forces to rise to the surface. A symbol changes our focus so deeply, that it removes old habitual patterns. Then, new patterns can emerge. The deeper the clearing, the more the mind opens to messages from the soul. Symbols facilitate a kind of psychic language. Where normal language and rational thinking can unravel the mind, tangle it, and even wrestle it to the ground, symbolic thinking opens the mind to the deeper mysteries.

The more we allow life to flow through us, the deeper the rearranging, and when we rearrange our house, we open up interior spaces that have been in stagnation. When we rearrange our minds, using symbolic metaphors, as in mythology, we open the subconscious to the light of the soul.

So Ellie, without myths and symbols are we psychically less enlightened as a culture?

Myths have been great evolutionary tools of the soul, allowing us to uncover what is beneath the surface of our consciousness. Asking the question, how one makes sense of a myth is [antithetical] to the meaning of myth in the first place. How can you make sense of a flower? Can you ask a flower, why do you exist? Myths are the psyche's freeways to higher consciousness. Travel the path of a myth and you will arrive without ever having left. You remain the same, while your perceptions of life change and deepen.

Are you saying that when we experience a myth, we are rearranging old mental and genetic patterns?

Yes, when you tell a myth you are rearranging old patterns and blueprints that do not serve you anymore.

When the same symbols appear repeatedly in different cultures and regions across the world, does that suggest we are all connected at the soul level?

Yes. More than we realize. As we are all learning, a creation myth explains how the world comes into being and establishes a creative process.

After hearing this from Ellie, I realized I would be able to co-create a story with my horses. To do this, I took a Shamanic journey to get in touch with my allies who would be helping me. I first wanted to write Buddy's personal soul myth. Then Buddy, Ellie, Dutch and I would shape a collection of equine creation myths together.

Using interspecies communication, I embarked on several storytelling experiments with the purpose of expanding my consciousness through the consciousness of my horses. We would explore the restorative power of myth together while employing telepathy between species.

The storytelling process, combined with the healing energy of animals, was a wonderful experience. Their stories opened spiritual pathways and helped me to reconnect with Mother Earth and the animals in a sacred way. Their myths taught me how to be in the world with more love and compassion while helping to reach into my ancestral past.

I conducted the storytelling process by merging with my horses mentally and spiritually. I knew the myths would help readers understand the spirit of the horse. I believe that myths are deeply embedded in the genetic code of all species on Earth. Rediscovering them became my life's work. The collective myths of Equus are compiled in the chapter titled "The New Myths of Equus." And Buddy's, Ellie's, and Dutch's personal soul myths follow.

Termas, Gong-ter and Tertons

While humanity is experiencing a significant and far-reaching reformation, both scientifically and spiritually, the West is still just beginning to experience what the East has known for thousands of years. Buddhist philosophies are spreading outward on a grand scale. The Dalai Lama travels and teaches, asking us to go to greater spiritual depths.

One custom I have come to cherish from the Tibetan tradition is called *terma*. It relates to a sacred object, text, or teaching that is hidden by the spiritual masters of one age for the benefit of a future generation in which the terma is found.

Tantric masters who discover terma are known as *Tertons* or treasure finders. The terma may be found in physical locations such as caves or cemeteries, or in elements such as water, wood, or earth. Terma can also be found in dreams and visionary experiences, as well as animals, trees, plants, or directly in deep levels of consciousness. The latter is called *gong-ter* or mind treasure.

Types of Terma

Francesca Fremantle, author of *Luminous Emptiness: Understanding the Tibetan Book of the Dead* confirms that according to Buddhist tradition:

"Termas are of two main kinds: Earth treasures and intention or mind treasures. A Teaching that is concealed as an intention treasure appears directly within the mind of the tertön in the form of sounds or letters to fulfill the enlightened intention. Earth treasures include not only texts, but sacred images, ritual instruments, and medicinal substances. These are found in temples, monuments, statues, mountains, rocks, trees, lakes, even the sky."

In the event one finds a written text, it is not an ordinary book that one can read. Occasionally, a person finds a full-length text, but it is often broken up. Occasionally the texts consist of only one or two encoded words in an allegorical script, which may change mysteriously and disappear entirely once it has been transcribed. These texts are simply the material supports that act as triggers to help a tertön reach the subtle levels of mind where the teaching has been concealed.

It is the tertön who actually composes and writes down the resulting text, and so may be considered the author.

The earth-terma are tangible objects—which may be actual texts or physical objects that trigger a recollection of the teaching. The mind-terma are constituted by space and are placed via guru-transmission. Terma can be a realization achieved in meditation that connects a practitioner directly with the necessary contents of the teaching in one simultaneous experience. Once this occurs, the tertön holds the complete teaching in his or her mind and is required by convention to transcribe the terma twice from memory in one uninterrupted session. The transcriptions are compared, and if no inconsistencies exist, the terma is sealed as authentic. Then the tertön must realize the essence of the terma prior to formal transmission.

In one sense, all terma are mind-terma because the teachings associated are always inserted in the mind of the practitioner. In other words, the terma are at all times a direct mind stream transmission. Also, the terma can be held in the mind stream of the tertön and realized in a future incarnation at a beneficial time.

A vision of a syllable or symbol can also trigger the

realization of a latent terma in the mind stream of a tertön. The process of hiding in the mind stream implies that the practitioner is to gain realization in that lifetime. At the time of terma concealment, a prophecy is made concerning the circumstances during which the teaching will be re-accessed. This is true in the case of an earth-terma. The prophecy includes a description of the place, and could specify tools or other objects needed, as well as any assistants who may accompany the tertön at the time of discovery.

Termas are not always made public as soon as they are discovered. Conditions may not be exactly right as people may not be ready, and further instructions may need to be revealed to the finder to clarify meaning. Often, the tertön has to practice them for many years.

For me, the following myths and stories, as told to me by my horses, are not a sentimental romancing of the past, but the rediscovery of hidden treasures found within the mind stream of equine consciousness. The following conversation with Buddy about the origin of myths is his way of introducing Section Two titled "The Mythology of Equus."

CHAPTER FIVE

Buddy on Myth

"I have spread my dreams under your feet. Tread softly because you tread on my dreams"

~ W. B. Yeats

One day a new student came to meet me and Buddy at our home in Hillsboro, Oregon. She had heard about us from a friend and wanted to meet the famous "talking" horse. Being a purebred Quarter Horse, Buddy not only impresses people with his psychic wisdom but with his muscular confirmation and gentle demeanor. His warmth goes beyond mere physicality. When standing in Buddy's presence people feel his soul.

My student had heard about my work with animal telepathy and wanted to ask Buddy a few questions about her own spiritual path. It was customary for me to give private readings in the barn with Buddy during the 1990s. We called his stall his office. I explained this little known fact to students while walking them up to the barn.

I would introduce new people to Buddy the same way every time. Then, he would telepathically inform me why the

student had come to see us, and what he or she wanted to know. Buddy did this even before the person had had a chance to speak.

In the case of this new person, Buddy insisted that I provide her with a stool to sit on in his stall. After sitting, he methodically bent over her shoulder and exhaled intentionally into her eyeglasses, fogging the left lens only. He did this in such a controlled way that it seemed odd to us. We laughed, thinking he was just being funny. But then he went over to the other side and fogged the other lens with just enough breath to fog the other lens. When he finished, both lenses were fogged and she could not see through her glasses at all. Then he stood back, watched and waited. It was typical for Buddy to be cryptic. He always knew how to make clients laugh with his antics. But, this time it was different.

Feeling humbled, my student immediately stood up and said, "I know what he is trying to tell me. He wants me to look within." She thanked him and said the message was meaningful to her.

Several years later, when she developed macular degeneration, she remembered Buddy's advice—to stop looking outside for answers and "see" within. This time Buddy's wisdom had deeper implications.

Buddy teaches with humor. He once told the same student to put "velcro on her [seat]" and stay put for a while. Again, she understood the message as she had been trying unsuccessfully to learn meditation. The image stayed with her and still makes her laugh.

A few years later, while preparing to write Buddy's personal soul myth, I asked him to tell me more about the process of Mythmaking. This is what he said:

Myths come from you and me. They come from all of us. We are living the myths of those who came before us. Until we awake from these old myths of yesterday, we are all still asleep.

In this context, I am using myth as synonymous with a lie. And there are many lies that people are living without knowing it. They must all wake up. The idea that animals do not communicate with humans is such a myth.

You learned that was not true many years ago. Keep thinking of other myths that are not true, and you will move forward. Open your heart and see what other myths you live by that are untrue. Take time to realize them and cast out them out so that you can grow.

Thank you, Buddy. Today, I am thinking of myths that are spiritually based, those that guide us and open our hearts.

In perfect stillness we were formed with thoughts---our own. The dimension you speak of called The Past, does linger into The Present, until you awaken from The Dream.

Awaken to what it is that you want to create in your life and you will find the roots of that dream in your myth of origin.

Do you mean that we look ahead to know what was seeded in us from the past?

Karma is just like that. Many seeds make many futures. That you can complete this book is good, it is a major seed in your mythology. So is Shamanism.

Buddy, tell me more about myth from your perspective.

A myth is the way back home. The roads we take are the stories we tell. All beings' myths are their avenues back home. When you tell a myth, you are going home. The myth takes you back in truth to love. A myth brings you back to the place of the Soul, and it is where your heart resides.

Why is the idea of home such a recurring theme in human culture? Are we not already home?

We are fixated on home because we are lost, wandering aimlessly, unaware of the truth, numb, afraid, feeling unloved, without warmth, light or a guiding fire inside.

When we tell a myth, do we rekindle the hearth fires that bring us back into alignment with our place of Oneness in the arms of the Mother/Father/Creator?

The Creator and the Created is also a myth simply because the mind cannot fathom Nothingness, which is where we all come from. Nothingness in human translation is the Void, Emptiness in Space between Times.

Emptiness is the Void?

Yes. That part of all myths is true. True for all forms. All life comes from the Sacred Dark Void.

What is beyond the Void?

The deepest level of mythology that humans can understand. This place is called the Genetic Memories.

How do we know the Genetic Memories exist?

We get glimpses in our Remembering Ceremonies. Remembering in a sacred way is a healing tool, and to remember the Void Beyond is coming back to us now. The Void is deep down in our bones and in our DNA. We all have been encoded with 'Remembering.' With these memories we can relive life and see it in holographs and multidimensional 'picture memories' that instruct and inform us about our sacred past.

Does your myth of origin go back to the Void?

We are not ready to go there now. Today, I want to start on the Earth. Myths are our common language---the energy of the soul. But so is a flower our common language, as is a song, or the dance of a killer whale, or the screech of an owl. These are all our common languages: The language of the Soul.

I want to tell you the story of our Common Soul. You are writing your works that come from your years of distillation of your many paths. It is your evolving story itself.

The Myth of the Horse--Did you think this would be a fairy tale? Myths are not trivial or light fairy tales.

I do not know what to expect. I expected something similar to what I have read about human myths. But this process feels different.

Our myths are going to include those myths of the nonhuman species. Mythology opens and expands the human heart. Maybe a myth is short and to the point, only a couple of sentences. Would you be disappointed?

No. I just need to become more familiar with the process. (As I wrote this, I heard Buddy whinny outside. When I got up, I saw him rubbing noses with Ellie in the pasture.)

We horses came to Earth as a group of souls who knew our mission and our purpose. Some of us are more on our purpose than others. We are all spiritual teachers and there are some who are like your Gurus too, your more highly adapted and evolved souls. I am an evolved leader among many. Ellie is too. Dutch follows, but he follows with his heart. He is heart-centered.

I believe I woke up to my soul myth when I met you.

We all remember when we woke up, if we did wake up at all. There are also those who are still asleep and who are beginning to awaken. Bless them and help them to awaken gently.

Section 2

The Mythology of Equus:

Part One

CHAPTER SIX

The New Myths of Equus

"Insight comes in when you don't dwell on things, or try to grasp at your own thoughts."

~ Pema Chodron.

We often find it difficult to understand and interpret the symbols and metaphors used in mythology. The reason is that we have to shift our consciousness back and forth, from left to right brain, to go with the flow---to build bridges between feeling and thought. Left-brain rules cognition, right brain rules creative, artistic expression.

When we do not understand a myth completely, we need to let go of it, and let insight come in. That is when new synapses fire in the brain, making fresh associations between seemingly disparate ideas. Myths are meant to be read figuratively, not literally.

As an animal communication specialist, I work with these ideas to teach people how to communicate telepathically with nonhuman nature. It is a lot like teaching people how to interpret symbols and metaphors in dreams. Once we understand the meaning of a symbol, we can better understand the dream or myth.

In other words, myths do not work according to Aristotelian logic, but instead to "fuzzy logic," where concepts and ideas are diffuse and indefinite. Myths, symbols, and dreams all work at the deeper levels of consciousness, and so does the process of animal communication. Westerners are not used to this kind of "fuzzy logic," which is how our ancestors told myths and communicated with animals and nature long ago.

Our difficulty in understanding myths and their hidden truths stems from the conflicts we experience when using our current language, between the use of words and images. We often say, "a picture is worth a thousand words," or "words cannot begin to describe." Words may define a subject directly, but images point to it and broadcast it so that each of us can interpret the meaning subjectively.

Language accustoms us to reason literally, where as symbolism works through the creative imagination. Buddhists use the expression, "You have to cook it," meaning to meditate on it, or contemplate it to understand the depth of it. Like poetry, myths can be difficult to grasp in a rational sense.

Working with the right brain, to move deeper into the mysteries of life, often feels uncomfortable for beginners because they must give up old mental conditioning. Yet working with the mind in this way can make us better able to focus and concentrate. It is the same as giving up an addiction. Those who want to be comfortable in life can forget being wise. Those who are attached to the small pleasures in life do not realize the bigger ones.

To enjoy the following myths and stories from Buddy, readers may need to "read between the lines" so to speak, or "suspend disbelief." Myths are not logical or rational. In an interview with Joseph Campbell by Tom Collins, called *Mythic Reflections,* in *In Context Magazine,* Campbell explains this:

"Myths put you in touch with a plane of reference that goes past your mind and into your very being, into your very gut. The ultimate mystery of being and nonbeing transcends all categories of knowledge and thought. The function of mythological symbols is to give you a sense of "Aha! Yes. I know what it is, it's me. This is what it's all about, and then you feel a kind of centering, centering, centering all the time. And whatever you do can be discussed in relationship to this ground of truth. Though to talk about it as truth is a little bit deceptive because when we think of truth we think of something that can be conceptualized. But myths go past that."

Campbell calls a symbol, "a sign that points past itself to a ground of meaning and being that is one with the consciousness of the beholder." Campbell notes that a myth is "transparent to the transcendent. If a deity blocks transcendency, cuts you short of it by stopping at himself, he turns you into a devotee. He hasn't opened the mystery of your own being. This is the function of mythology, to be transparent to the transcendent."

In subsequent chapters, we will build bridges between the conscious and unconscious mind to understand myths and recognize their transcendent meaning. This understanding will help students of animal communication begin to relate to animal wisdom by deepening intuition, telepathy, and empathy. This experiential learning is a dynamic pathway to higher consciousness. It raises conscious awareness to a higher level.

Buddy based the following creation myths for horses on the Hindu Chakra System---one creation myth for each of the seven Chakras. He calls them "The New Myths of Equus."[5] (For those who need more of a foundation about the Chakra System please refer to Anodea Judith's book, *"The Wheels of Life: A User's Guide to the Chakra System."*)

Myth One: The Root Chakra
Myth of Equus and the Earth

Affirmation for the First Chakra: I am rooted in the power of stillness.

The First Chakra relates to our physical energies. Since we are the creators of our own experiences, we need to be grounded in the physical world with a healthy Root Chakra. Manifestation on the physical plane requires us to be in the present moment and to be energetically aware of our bodies. Buddy begins this chapter by telling a myth about horses concerning the Chakra of Manifestation.

When I asked him to talk about creation myths for the species Equus, he began by showing me the Chakra System as a range of sounds, vibrational frequencies, colors, images, voices, rhythms, and movements. He said the Chakra System is a synergy of these energies, and that this synergy creates form—all form and matter on Earth.

Myths are the connective tissue of the spiritual life. Myths come from the spiritual realm. To find your personal connection to `spirit is to find your personal soul myth.

We were once "Travelers" who moved across the face of this

―――――――――――――――――

[5] For those who need more of a foundation about the Chakra System please refer to Anodea Judith's book, *"The Wheels of Life: A User's Guide to the Chakra System.*

vast universe. Horses were formless travelers. They were formless energies looking for meaning and purpose. There were also Travelers who knew their meaning and purpose, who were also looking for form.

Cosmic energy seeks to express itself in form on Earth. All matter has a soul myth. And this soul myth reflects the basic synergies of life. It encompasses all form and formless beings, no matter who, or what, or where.

Your soul myth is your guiding myth. Your soul myth is your "pilot" myth, guiding your energies into form. Your soul is the central processor, the captain of your vessel. If you know how to ride the soul, you can create anything in the world, and bring what you want to create into manifestation. The soul is at the center, like a nucleus at the center of a cell. When the cell divides and multiplies, this is because all cells have connected at the center, equally. The force of that connection breaks the cell in half and where there was one there are now two. And, so on. LIFE HAPPENS!

The "driving force" or "soul" of the Traveler is free to choose its own organization or organizing pattern. Once the "force" gains consensus from the collective that is when something starts to "materialize." It is the law of the universe at work creating matter. The laws of attraction bring simple organisms into contact with each other and then you have a group energy or "mind."

The Travelers are those who have broken free from their original forms and are looking for complimentary Travelers to connect with. Once they have a collective agreement, and enough capacity and force, then comes movement. Once there is enough momentum, through collective movement, then comes speed, and higher velocity, and so on.

Those who keep true to their original form stay with the movement. Those who cannot stay true, either leave, or die. This is how species are born, or exit--through purpose, momentum, speed *and velocity, (momentum relates to purpose, relates to consensus, relates to force, relates to mass.)*

What we see and call horses today, were once Sky Travelers in an infinite universe of possibilities. The Earth, being a small, but powerful force, attracts certain energies to itself.

These energies recruit other Travelers who choose to respond, or not. But once there is enough momentum, and the momentum takes hold, it is hard to turn back. So, one must be careful to choose which force to move with.

As you get closer, things start to go faster and faster, until the manifestation process is complete. The force gathers mass like a snowball rolling downhill.

Now, to return to your question and how it relates to the Chakra of Manifestation. When all energies agree, all forces are working in harmony. That is when the Traveler breaks through into form.

The horse, as a form, was originally like all other forms of its kind (mammals). It was not strong or weak. The horse was small and happy to have an Earthly experience. But as time moved on, the horse adapted to the needs of the Earth. The overriding species, the master species, always prevailed. The master species is the one species that adapts most quickly to the ever-changing environment.

Then, the word went out that new forms were coming in, and the old forms (dinosaurs) were fading out. Size and mass does matter, because at some point form become unsustainable.

But then came the Announcement. The Announcement came when all the energies were properly assembled and organized into patterns. Growth is like an announcement to the world.

Horses heard the spiritual Announcement from the other Travelers in the long line of Creation. Creation is a continual line of manifestation as well as destruction.

106

When the horses heard the Announcement, each one had a choice to make. They could move into the next phase of their species' growth, (evolution) or they could opt out, (extinction.)

So when the horses heard the Announcement, some agreed to evolve, and others opted out. Each one had their own independent choice to make. However, once they chose, they had to faithfully fulfill their contract.

What was/is the contract? As the Earth evolved, horses' contract with Spirit was more Earth-centered, meaning they could stay on the Earth as long as they did not harm other life forms, and if they agreed to make a contribution of some kind to life on Earth. Their contribution, it turns out, was to humanity.

So when the horses kept their contract, they were promised continual life on Earth and a space to fill. But if they broke their contract or their promise, then they would have to return to the "soup of creation." And then they were free to start over again.

Today, horses are trying hard to stay on this planet. Their habitats are shrinking in vast amounts and since they no longer have jobs as powerful movers, their work is limited.

The jobless rate for horses today is fast approaching ninety percent. That means that ninety percent of all horses on Earth have no meaningful work. They are out of a job and face losing their home planet Earth.

Therefore, instead of working in the physical world to keep their contract, as warhorses or for transportation, horses are here to answer another call, advancement/Announcement. That is to help humans focus on their human spiritual contract with the Earth. This contract is to do no harm, and make the Earth good for all, and to help the Earth support all life forms. Humans have become greedy and self-centered. They are being asked to learn how to share their space and life together. To share their resources--air, water and land, with each other.

Horses are altruistic in nature. They share with each other as long as no one gets hurt. They will defend themselves when needed, but they prefer nonviolence.

The essential message of our myth today for the human race for the Chakra of Manifestation is one of NONVIOLENCE.

"Object to violence because when it appears to do good, the good is only temporary; the evil it does is permanent." ~ Mohandas K. Gandhi

Myth Two: The Sacral Chakra
Myth of the Avatar

Affirmation: Life is pleasurable.

We began our mythic journey with the story and idea that matter and consciousness exist at opposite ends of the spectrum, generating the forces of creation.

Buddy began, in the first myth, by relating to the Root Chakra. In this, the second myth, the way to higher consciousness leads us first down through the waters of the Second Chakra. Through movement and change, desire, pleasure and the polarity of opposites, the forces of matter and consciousness are united. It is from the perpetual attraction and interaction of male and female energies, yin and yang, in the Second Chakra, that physical existence comes into being.

The polarities creating the motion of pushing and pulling are essential ingredients of energy, matter and consciousness. Without movement, life becomes stale. Creative motion brings the sweetness of life into the abdomen/womb from the place of stillness--the First Chakra.

When I asked Buddy to tell a creation myth for Equus

relating to the Second Chakra, he took me flying over an ocean dotted with jewel green islands. I could feel the spray of the waves touching my face as I viewed everything below in close detail.

This is the island where ancient horses once roamed free as the wind. We could fly, swim, or run as we wished. We feasted on manna from heaven, and life was good.

When I asked how horses came to this place, he showed me ships that looked like islands in the water. Perhaps these islands were at one time joined but later were separated by the rising tides.

When horses wanted to swim, they could join in a circular dance and dive deeply into the water together. Then, we transformed ourselves so that we could breathe under water where we could visit our "generating" force. We called that force "Black Mud." Black Mud had much to teach us about the powers of purification and soul growth. Black Mud lived at the center of the Earth, inside the core. But when Black Mud knew horse spirits were coming, he would step out to greet us at the gate and show us inside.

The fires burning inside the core were intensely hot and brought horses to their knees. However, once the horses were prepared, we would sit in counsel with Black Mud and listen to the stories he wished to tell. We talked about our mission on Earth and once we received our orders, we would flow back up to the Earth's surface and move across the land like lava. We would make ourselves known all over the world, even to those in the sky. Like Black Mud when he came to the surface, we too flowed far and wide.

News of our spiritual powers spread for many generations on the islands. We could live more than one hundred years. But the islands were crossed with the blood of those who wanted to capture us, and own us for our powers.

We were known throughout the land by those who could ride

us. They called us Avatars.

Later, I looked up the word Avatar. It stems from Sanskrit meaning descent, as in descent from heaven to earth, or to cross over, which implies a deliberate line of descent from the spiritual realms to the lower realms for special purposes.

A rider who could stay seated on the back of an Avatar horse for the longest time would live many consecutive lifetimes. He could not die except in his bed of old age. He would not suffer injury in any battle or die on any battlefield. Great battles were fought to possess an Avatar horse.

One day, during a spiritual festival on the island, the highest warrior vowed to get hold of one of the Avatars for his daughter, Lumina. He wanted her to live forever and never be touched by the slightest shadow of death.

Yet in order to own a horse of this magnificent stature, Lumina had to learn to capture the heart of the beast herself. She went through many challenges to learn her lessons. Finally one day, when she was ready, she started on her journey to find the Avatar of her dreams. When she came upon the horse lying beside a lake, restoring his strength in the stillness there, she was elated. But unknown to her, her enemies had also sent out warriors to capture this illustrious horse.

Suddenly, the dark spirits of the lake released by the movement of her enemies caught the horse up and a great battle ensued. The horse fought bravely and held the enemy off for a time. But in the end, taking the Avatar's last bit of strength, the enemy threw the horse into the depths of the lake, denying Lumina her long-awaited prize.

As this occurred, a great monster with huge tentacles erupted from the surface of the lake and captured the horse in its mouth before plunging back into the pitch-dark waters. According to the myth, the horse lies there still, in the belly of the beast, awaiting

110

redemption from his Lady Lumina.

In the present day, when the moon is full and the powers of the feminine psyche are on the rise, Lumina, now a beautiful Queen with shimmering red hair and striking green eyes, can be seen on her throne in her island paradise dreaming of the day when she will rescue her Avatar from his deep sleep. She is said to be a Virgin Bride, gathering her feminine powers to return to the lake one day to bring the Avatar back to life from its depths.

The Avatar horse can only return when Lumina dives into the lake and rides him through the dark waters, into the world again. When she rides him, he becomes a white unicorn who can fly. From that point, he can only be ridden by a winged Goddess whose name is Peace Rocking Horse.

Buddy and Ellie together told the ending to the story of the Winged Goddess, Peace Rocking Horse:

Peace Rocking Horse has many winds that guide her through her life. The wind of grace gives her compassion when she feels tender. The wind of trust helps when she is drained and out of balance with her brothers and sisters.

Peace Rocking Horse's shadow sways back and forth on a shimmering ocean of light. Her eyes are like the deep blue waters. In the night, against a vast star-field, inside the dream of the Earth, Peace Rocking Horse rocks gently back and forth, weaving her prayers into colorful patterns, embracing the mountains of the Earth with the moisture of change.

Slowly, oceanic waves swell inside her womb from rocking, feeding her spirit with joy. Peace Rocking Horse seeds her womb with love as the rolling waves of her joyful heart lull the seeds with a calming hush. One by one, the seeds descend into Earth's soft clay to await their moment of rebirth.

Peace Rocking Horse is full with movement, rhythm, motion, and gathering. She soothes the sharp edges of our lives with gentle rocking motion. She melts the iron core of humans as the ebb and flow of her sweet milk nourishes the human spirit. She is the Goddess Mother who births the Avatar horse.

Myth Three: The Solar Plexus
Myth of the Crystal Horse

Affirmation: I claim my personal power and accept responsibility for all areas of my life.

This affirmation helps us to maintain a healthy and balanced Third Chakra. The Third Chakra is about power and self-understanding. It is about listening to internal guidance and wisdom. It is also where animals and humans respond to their gut feelings, intuition and instincts.

Earth, water, fire. With our bodies grounded and our emotions flowing, we are ready to move into our personal power with right action, energy, and willpower. The fire of life in the belly is where the spark ignites the will to action. Fire is the spark that rests between the poles, and the Third Chakra creates that combustive power from the tension of opposites introduced by the Second Chakra. The Third Chakra is the place of dynamic balance between these two extremes.

As I tuned into Buddy for this Third Chakra myth, I saw an image of humans energetically dancing with horses through a connection between their power centers––at the level of the solar plexus. For humans, some of these ancient past-life memories are stored in the Third Chakra and they can be difficult emotionally to remember and ultimately to release. Some of the Third Chakra material, relating to horses, represents humanity's darkest hour with the spirit of the horse.

When I asked Buddy to tell a myth about horses relating to the Third Chakra, he told the following story:

A relationship of power between humans and horses began when civilizations moved across the face of the Earth in huge migrations on horseback. The myth from ancient Greece of horses pulling the sun across the sky in a golden chariot refers to the idea that horses and humans embrace their personal sovereignty together. The will of the people to be self-governing is manifested with the aid of the horse.

Having taken another step toward higher consciousness, humans tempered their desire and instincts with increased knowledge and they made decisions, which they put into action by combining the opposite poles of mind and body.

Millions of years have gone into creating the herd instinct that limits an individual horse's freedom. The herd instinct is a reaction born of the fear of the potential harm an individual horse's actions can have on the herd as a whole. That which is born in fear, blossoms into judgment, stubbornness, and even violence. This ancient and virtually autonomic reaction does not allow us, as a species, to evolve as individuals easily.

The horse you know today was "created" and shaped by the will of humans to use our strength and speed. We never wanted to go to war or to surrender to human greed. But that was a part of our evolutionary plan. We were pounded and shaped like steel around the anvil of human tenacity — through fire and force.

Humans forced their will on the horse, but the will of the horse was equal to yours, and so this battle-dance of power became the foundation of our long-held destiny and relationship with you. Human methods of control and contact with us were ingenious. You developed many ways of dis-empowering us—-the horse you also loved.

You remember only a few short years ago, people thought

they needed to train horses with extreme force (the negative side of human will). Some horses gave way to this power struggle. Some resisted unto death.

The male horse was always a stallion then. It was a time before humans learned how to denature horses. We were full in our power and speed. When humans learned to temper the horse's power with their own strength, that is when horses, as you know us today, were created.

This was a time when people and horses resisted each other through their will power, through the push and pull and struggle of selves. We were never one with humans through force.

You are still learning this between yourselves. It was always about surrender for us to survive. We had to surrender if we wanted to live with humans. Once surrendered, a "broken" horse was never the same. Our evolution diverged there.

Humans used fire to create fear in us, to make us bow. This was also the fire power between human souls at battle with each other. It has been a dance of suffering. One that persists. When the horse learned to give to humans, we had no love, no peace, and no connection in our hearts. This made us live in shame and fear and sadness, even deep depression. Then came the gelding process. The final humiliation.

A story to show this idea might go like this:

The sun is slowly emerging from beneath a distant horizon. The deafening sounds of a thousand hoof beats thunder across a barren landscape. Dark clouds of red dust reflect in the thick mists of dawn, igniting a fire in the center of your physical power. As a spiritual warrior, you are poised to engage in battle on horseback.

Ritualistically, you groom your horse, fitting him for the conflict. You arm his feet with fire and steel. They are the weapons of war. Next, you suit him with breast and nose plate and drape his flanks with leather.

The guilt of your actions genetically remains a stain for most of you in your solar plexus. Our desire, our love of power and speed and strength is what we traded with you to survive. We must fight to regain that spiritual power and renew our spiritual position on Earth.

Humans manifested a "submitting beast" from the force of their will. We were your protection from our mutual understanding of what power meant in the world. How you manifest your firelight in the coming days, through flashes of will and energy, will allow you to relinquish your "energy stain" and guilt. The fires that kept us together through storm, water, and wind, are returning to Earth in the New Era.

As we enter a New Era, one in which the flow of cosmic fire is pouring onto Earth and growing more intense, the danger is that the inner fire will merge with the volatile energies within the Earth and cause earthquakes and other upheavals. This can be exacerbated by humans' misuse of fire, including the subtler fire of thoughts and feelings.

The energy bound by our karmic imprints from our dark emotions must be recycled at the level of the Third Chakra. When we let go of fear and anger, we reprogram the first three Chakras and allow them to deliver the life force we need in our quest for self-knowledge and healing.

Myth Four: The Heart Chakra
Little Dog, Big Dog ~ Guardian of Tears

Affirmation: I freely and easily give and receive love. I totally forgive others and myself for all past errors and judgments.

The Fourth Chakra is found in our heart center. It governs our intuition and love. The glands and organs of the body associated with this Chakra are the thymus, heart, lungs, chest, arms, and hands. The element is air and breathing exercises are helpful to keep this Chakra balanced. The emotion of the Heart Chakra is compassion and joy. When unbalanced, we can experience feelings of loneliness and the inability to forgive or empathize. A powerful way to energize this Chakra is to treat others consciously as we would have them treat us.

When I asked Buddy to tell a myth relating to this Chakra, he said:

All That Is saw so much human suffering on Earth and knew that something had to be done to help them. So All That Is plucked an eye out of the sky and sent the eye down to roam across the Earth to look for helpers who were willing to aid the humans in their struggle for peace.

The eye roamed far and cried many tears when it witnessed human suffering. It cried many tears for the children who were left to fend for themselves. The eye saw that the children needed to find their joy again. So the eye got itself swallowed by a little dog, and when the eye reached the dog's belly, the dog barked and laughed and began to play with the children. Then the children were happy again, and the dog looked over at the people, and the eye saw from inside its stomach that the people were also sad. But when the little dog tried to cheer them up, they complained about their heavy burdens. "We cannot dance across the land and carry our food and shelter and clothing. Our children are struck with the heavy weight."

"Oh," said the little dog, "I see from inside of me that the inside of you is sad and feels burdened. I will ask All That Is if we dogs can get bigger and stronger so we can carry your burdens for you." Then, the little dogs went off into the woods . . . but sadly they never returned.

116

Eons later, many dogs were coming out of the deep woods and their legs were long and their backs were strong and they had big muscled necks and heavy heads with teeth ten times the size of the little dogs. And the people were amazed. They remembered what the little dogs had said, and how the little dogs were kind and wanted to help them. So they wondered if the big dogs felt the same way as the little dogs once felt.. They tried to get close to the big dogs. But each time they tried, the big dogs just ran back into the woods.

One day, a big dog was lying on the ground with a little dog by its side. The little dog was sad because the big dog was dying. So, the humans took pity on the little dog and decided to feed it some milk from their goat. Then the little dog got bigger and bigger and one day the humans asked the big dog if it would carry one of their children. The big dog said, "Yes, you helped me when I was small and helpless so I will help you because you are also small and helpless. You need my strong back, my long legs, and my big muscles.

And so it was how little dogs who came to be big helped the people, and their hearts have been one ever since.

Myths Five, Six and Seven:
Throat, Third Eye and Crown Chakras
The Shining Harmonies of Equus

Affirmation for the Fifth Chakra: I easily and gracefully express my deepest feelings and emotions.

Affirmation for the Sixth Chakra: I see all things in clarity.

Affirmation for the Seventh Chakra: I am guided by a higher power.

The Fifth Chakra relates to the throat area in the V of the collarbone. It is the center of communication, sound, and expression of creativity through sound, speech, and writing. The possibility for transformation and healing are in this area of the body. The Sixth Chakra relates to the third eye, located above the physical eyes. It is the Chakra for psychic ability, higher intuition and energies of spirit and light. It helps in the purification of negative tendencies and in the elimination of selfish attitudes. The Seventh Chakra relates to the Crown, located above the top of the head. It is the center of spirituality, enlightenment, dynamic thinking and higher energies. It allows the inward flow of wisdom and brings the gifts of cosmic consciousness. This center is also the area of connectedness with God/Goddess, and is where life force animates the body.

When I asked Buddy to tell a Chakra myth for the next Chakra, he said he would combine the Firth, Sixth and Seventh Chakras into one myth. He mentioned this myth would show a connection for horses to Lemuria and Atlantis. So I asked him if horses had once lived there.

A long time ago, before the Great Flood, and for thousands of years before Lemuria, horses existed on the Earth as they do today. A paradise of amazing proportions rose up from the ocean floor. The land itself consisted of mountains and valleys floating like islands in the sea. We also had islands floating in the air as you have seen in your movie "Avatar." (Pandora is based on memory-pictures that are returning to human consciousness from your own past lives in Lemuria and Atlantis.)

The air was so thick that all life forms could fly through it at will. All that they needed was the will and the power to visualize. The visualization was not a fabricated projection, but the brain's ability, under concentration, to "see" what it cannot normally see, but is there in higher vibrational form. That is why it is so important

118

not to poison yourself with toxic food and water. The body needs clean nourishment to allow these higher vibrations to come through you as ALL THAT IS.

In Lemuria, the power to move objects and heavy matter was a gift that everyone knew and enjoyed. As you have polluted the Earth, air, water and your own bodies, these extraordinary abilities have receded into the background as latent potential. Yet, the mind can still recall and receive the abilities with intention, practice, purification and knowledge.

Raising your vibration again to allow yourselves to recover these powers will take time. Hundreds of years may pass before the human race will be ready and able to regain these abilities again. You are just now at the fount of re-wisening or re-wisdoming your brothers and sisters who will become triggered by your words and pictures.

To relive these memories, we will create a past life television, a high definition TV in our minds. The power supply is in your ancestral DNA—your cellular memories that contain "light" recordings. Once projected onto a screen in your mind, you can reanimate these light images by asking questions and waiting for answers that will be displayed on your mind-screen. Let's try it.

To set up your past life TV, let's decide which time you want to rediscover. You are asking about Lemuria, so let's set our screen to 800, 000 B.C.E. We will set our dial and start the tuning process. Just like finding a clear, strong signal on a radio, analog style, this will take patient listening skills. But it's the same process. So close your eyes and tune your whole body.

We will start in the present moment and tune our visual screens first. We are traveling to a remote island in what today you call the Pacific Ocean. The sea and land masses are unrecognizable from above because the land has moved. The former landmasses are now covered by water. As we tune into to our vision, we are flying

119

overhead in a "light" craft, also unrecognizable to your present day awareness. We are sitting in our craft as we slowly descend to the island of Lemuria.

Dolphins greet us at the dock. We come down gently into the water as the dolphins create a bridge that caries us across the water. The dolphins ask us to swim with them and we do so in a playful welcoming dance.

Now, instead of watching a TV screen we are going to go inside the scene. We are no longer viewing ourselves as separate, but instead we are participating in our own vision.

Once on the ground, we walk/glide into the jungle where the plant life, similar to the luminous plants on Pandora, come to greet us. We have a welcoming party with trees and flowers. There are brightly colored bird-like creatures flying as light-forms too. We are Bio-light forms---not at all solid. Our bodies are only semi-solid. I call this Bio-Light Plasma---you are tall, bipedal forms with translucent aqua-green skin.

Look at your hands, arms, and legs. You are as you are today, but today you are living with density and heaviness. You are attached to the Earth, slow, and plodding and in need of assistance to move around the planet with cars, planes, trains, and other forms of transportation, which are not needed in Lemuria.

We did not need Earthly inventions when we first arrived on this planet. Transportation was achieved with the mind. Transportation was like breathing is for you today. It came naturally, reflexively. It just happened. We also could move across vast expanses unaided by machines.

Can you imagine something like an iron lung attached to your mouth to help you breathe? In the future, you may not be walking unaided, but will only be able to move with a vehicle. You will have to use a machine to do your breathing for you because you will have become so reliant on machines. You will not be able to *breathe on your own because the air will also need to be purified for you. You will forget how to breathe on your own and your body will refuse to exchange polluted air and the toxins that are airborne. The breathing machines will be for the privileged few. The rest of humankind will suffer shorter life spans more and more. Living forever is not a fairy tale someone once told when you were young. Living forever in eternal bliss was a reality for ancient beings of the universe.*

On the main island, we explore what the dolphins call 'join-up' life forms of early Earth. It will be like going to the fun house at an amusement park, only this is within our reach in the jungle.

We watch the first of our party connect, just as they do on Pandora. We will be connected to a life form to experience what it experiences. Let us connect with a flowering tree for some interesting sensations during a rainstorm. We connect as the branches of the tree entangle themselves around our bodies.

The rain starts falling, filling the cavities in the branches, leaves and bark of the trees. It soaks into our shared skin. Then, it begins to trickle down our necks/trunks, tickling our toes/roots. Where the rain fills the upper layer of Earth, we siphon it back up through our feet/roots and our branches/arms, and leaves/hands. We are now a continuous waterfall of running water/energy. An unbroken circuit of etheric rain/energy is flowing through us from above, and we feel rejuvenated.

Now we are ready to experience the creatures most like horses that you know today. The horse in Lemuria is ten times larger than on Earth today. These animals eat rocks, dirt/earth, trees, whatever they want to eat because they are so big and strong. Their power is enormous. They do not swallow their food. They only have to put it in their mouths and allow the energy of the thing to become absorbed. They take the life force from it, and then place it back where they found it. Sometimes others must be careful because a piece of food can become depleted of life force and needs time to revitalize itself.

They place what they like on their skin, in their mouths or just hold it close to receive the elements from the etheric energy. But they do not ingest the Earth matter. Matter is too dense for the etheric beings.

We use our mouths for breathing and to make vocalizations. When we vocalize loudly, we can create storms. We can change the whole weather system with our sound. This was a way for warring entities to send us the "bad" energy they had collected by "overeating" the material things, and over-absorbing the etheric energy. They would get too involved with matter so that their Earth experience became heavy and dark. We had to "swallow" what they sent sometimes and it would make us feel ungrounded to our core. It would make us act and do crazy things. Sometimes we would disintegrate and not be able to recover. It was what you call death. We became dis-informed about our life force. Our etheric electrical impulses would become disintegrated. These impulses would go down into the Earth. Sometimes, if someone excavated the land where a large catastrophe like this had happened, where many of us had disintegrated in one place, the energy of that event, the energy that could not hold its center, was still inside the Earth. It would come back up to the surface and wreak havoc on the present environment. That type of dis-integrated electrical force does not dissipate. It can be reused if one knows how to reorganize it.

So the big Lemuria horse that looked like the horse you know today was unruly. They were not as peaceful as some other creatures; like the whales or dolphins that lived in the water that could swim all over the world unimpeded. The giant horse was unfulfilled on Earth because it was wildly voracious for meaning and purpose. It had no business there.

There was a time when human-like creatures were trying to

heal/tame the big horse creatures when an explosion occurred on the Earth. All the life forms were destroyed and everyone had to start over again, including the plant and animal life.

Sadly, an explosion, floods, and many fires destroyed Lemuria. None had time to return to use their light crafts and they were destroyed too. All life was left in limbo . . . until now.

There was no such thing as reincarnation for us because we were not incarnate in the first place. So the devastation merely brought us to a place of hibernation. The only way we could return to Earth was by coming out of hibernation or by coming back from what you call extinction. However, there was no such thing as extinction. Everything everywhere was eternal and there was no death, just a disorganization event, followed by a reorganization event.

If we find the right song/harmony and tone/vibration that could reorganize our species, we could come back to life again.

We can teach humans how to live eternally. Even in their Bio-Light forms. However, the mind will need to change. You will need to live from your light, vibration, sound, and other etheric energies and give up your love of density to feel alive on planet Earth. Density is not how you live in eternal glory.

The next time you put food or water in your mouth, remember the easiest density to ingest for your race is the nutrients in your minerals. But your bodies have evolved to use all matter on Earth and so you cannot deny this. For now, density it is. For now, you eat the flesh of other dense Earth creatures until you become disintegrated by the lower vibrations of these creatures. They will pull you out of your true vibrational frequency, which is light and sound, color, and patterns of these together. All life functions from these basic geometric grids and patterns; life seeks its release by letting go of the Earth density, eventually.

CHAPTER SEVEN

Buddy's Soul Myth:
Bodhisattva-Buddy Sattva

"It is possible that the next Buddha will not take the form of an individual. The next Buddha may take the form of a community--a community practicing understanding and loving kindness--a community practicing mindful living. This may be the most important thing we can do for the survival of the Earth."

~ Thich Nhat Hanh

In Buddhist thought, a Bodhisattva is someone who is dedicated to helping all sentient beings in achieving complete Buddhahood. Conventionally, the title applies to hypothetical beings with a high degree of enlightenment. The term Bodhisattva in Sanskrit means enlightenment (*bodhi*) and being (*Sattva*).

A Bodhisattva can be born as a human being or as an animal, and is distinguished from other beings by the certainty that eventually, after many lives, the Bodhisattva will be reborn as Buddha. Advanced Bodhisattvas can manifest in a great variety of forms, including devas, depending upon the circumstances.

As I began to meditate on transcribing Buddy's soul myth, he reminded me to see a myth as a metaphor, and not to take his story literally.

Then, I begin to see bubbles in a cauldron and someone stirring thick goo in a huge pot. I realize that someone is me and I continue stirring, round and round. Then, my Earthly body falls away as my spirit rises and takes off into the sky. Now, free and weightless, I gaze at the Earth where I see my horses grazing in the pasture by our house. I fall back to the Earth and stand invisible next to my horse, Buddy. We connect eye to eye, soul to soul. He looks at me from the side of his eye and he lets me into his vision. I then see the world from his view. It is a rich world of comfort and joy and grounded with deep, rich, spiritually bright, enhanced colors.

Once inside Buddy's mind, I ask to be shown his soul myth script. Then, someone comes up to me and I feel he is an usher of sorts. He escorts me into a dimly lit room. There is one light over a table with one chair. I sit at the table and see a book opened to the first chapter. It is called Buddy Sattva. Buddy smiles and winks at me. I laugh. I know I am on the right track because Buddy uses humor to teach. We never take ourselves too seriously.

I turn to the first page of the chapter called Buddy Sattva and, as I do, I see moving images across the page, not words, directing my thoughts. I see several railroad trains coming from all points, arriving at a central station. The trains are bringing the wisest old souls to be together again. The trains stop and out come many beings. One of them is me in a previous human form. One is Buddy. He is a doctor of human medicine.

I hear Buddy say:

This is my soul's awakening time, about two hundred years ago. I had rested on the train so I was ready to work. I am traveling with a child (you), I take her hand, and we walk to a house. I make a fire and we sit and eat. I look into her eyes and for the first time she sees me for who I really am. We are drawn to the fire and our human emotions of father and child share comfort, warmth, curiosity and letting go. I begin to tell her the story of my soul myth.

 *The horses of old had big, smiling hearts. I sprang from my mother's smiling heart. A gleam, a twinkle, a shining moment. I inhabited her heart for many years until her death. Then I lost my way and I wandered. I almost died too. But then I awakened to my song and I hummed myself back to life.*

My soul myth is the story of all the recorded teachings from Tibet told by monks and high lamas. I was a stone in a Tibetan monastery. I recorded every prayer that was ever spoken for hundreds and hundreds of years. The stones in the monastery carry vibrations and memories. One day, those prayers created a life. The stones created a life from the energy of the prayers they held and absorbed. I came from the clay and straw of that cornerstone. I was a cornerstone in a monastery. I upheld the vows and wisdom of the Buddha until one day I was one too. I glow in the dark. If you look closely, you will see that you do too. That is your wisdom light shining through. You too are like a rock, recording all that is, and one day you will transform as I did. My wisdom showed me how to put my light, and my prayers into a woman and she gave birth to a child. That child carries the stories you are now telling because that child is you. My life as a cornerstone was designed to receive love while upholding a tradition. That tradition is the foundation of my life. I am born of this foundation and this tradition. I uphold all that is true

for you and for the world. You can rely on me, lean on me, depend on me. I am your rock, your father, your truth, your world.

My soul sprang from the prayers I recorded in my heart. A cornerstone is unmovable. If you remove a cornerstone, the structure will collapse. I am attuned to that eternal, unmoving strength and power upon which all else is built. I am all that is under in understanding. It is like when you sit with a dying person, and that person's soul comes to the surface, and is at peace. I am that peace, that strength, that rock that upholds perfect love for the universe. I am one with perfect love and absolute peace. As a cloud drifts overhead gathering rain, I am a rock in a monastery, unmoving, gathering love. From that love comes total peace.

The peace of centuries is inscribed inside of me. I am there, now, in the past, and forever. I am what Jesus taught, what the Buddha knows. Now you know too. Congratulations. You have touched a cornerstone. You have talked with a cornerstone from a monastery. Be wise. Be well.

CHAPTER EIGHT

Buddy on Atlantis:
Shapeshifters in Antiquity

While writing one day, Buddy announced that he remembered a personal lifetime in Atlantis. This intrigued me, so I asked him to tell me more.

My soul group was stationed there for many years. The sport of horse racing also started in Atlantis.

Can you say more about what it was like then? Were you a horse?

I was with several species then. We could shapeshift ourselves at will. I was a human, I was wind, I was horse, I was mountain, and I was bird. I could shapeshift into any and all of these all the time. I was one with the message these beings bring in knowledge to create joy for all.

What was it like to live in Atlantis as a horse, human, wind, mountain, and bird? How can one be so many things simultaneously?"

Being part human for a horse is easy. We walk on two legs and stand upright. It is a thrill for us whose spines are normally vertical to the ground. Then, the energy surges up our spines, even though it takes some effort to sustain this posture. When stallions go to battle, they often posture for supremacy in this way.

Does this upright posture lend supremacy to humans too?

No, only the four-leggeds. Because four-leggeds could not survive on two legs. We realize there is power using our front legs for warring while balancing on two. It stretches the capabilities of four-legged creatures. But four-leggeds could not survive on two legs.

Stallions in the wild are in this upright position for breeding. Is that why?

Yes, it stretches our capabilities.

So, how does it feel being part human/part horse on two legs on a mountaintop in the wind?

The wind is freeing. I feel free on two legs, with flight like a bird over a mountaintop. All those things come together in the moment.

We share those moments with each other: Wind, bird, horse, human and mountain. Many feel this combination is a good one. You may have seen us in your picture books. We appear as humans on horseback under a big sky on a wide-open mountain range. That is what we call Shapeshifting.

I see. When you put it that way, I see the whole is greater than its parts. It is interesting to think of it that way. Tell me more about your relationship with humans in Atlantis.

My relationship with humans as a horse was based on total freedom. The humans worshiped the spiritedness of horses and never wanted to denature them as they do today. The more freedom the horses had the better we were. They revered us for our speed of flight and our unsurpassed joy in running.

Horse racing began in Atlantis, where horses and humans first became aware of the bond you call domestication. It began as a 'riderless' race. Horses were asked to race against each other by their human counterparts. We had complete respect between species then. Horses were never "tamed," and humans did not try to capture us. We agreed to perform for you, but only from a distance.

Tell me about horse racing? What did that entail?

We were given a period in which we were asked to run — a day, week, month — often through water and over mountains. We ran for the sheer pleasure and joy of it. The horse who made it to the final destination first became the herd leader. If he were a stallion, he would take several mares and a few of younger males and start his own herd.

Was that like a Rite of Passage for horses?

Yes, and more. The humans already knew this behavior was pure to horses so we naturally fulfilled these races.

Like human families who expand and start their own families, we too migrated over countless miles always on the alert for what the environment had to teach us. We "raced" for many centuries and the people watched us, named us, counted us, and speculated on us, wondering which of us would come in ahead of the herd, as you do today. Only we were free back then.

We entered this relationship with humans by choice, out of mutual honor and respect, and because there might be a higher purpose too--something we did not know much about. We sensed it was an important bond--important to the higher ideals of both horses and humans. And that is how we became acquainted with humans too.

We have a highly developed horse/human culture in the world today. It is very strong and I am proud of our accomplishments. But some horses do not fully enjoy this development. Humans have enslaved the horse, and horses have allowed themselves to become enslaved to humans. This is not the honored position we would take if we had a choice. This is the dark side of this development. Those who wanted only to race for their own sense of freedom were self-serving and never understood the higher plan, the larger plan.

Let's try a Shapeshifting exercise so you can experience the joy of other elements and species. Go ahead and listen to your heart. What different shapes would you be, if you could be anything at all?

I would be a dolphin, a flower fairy, and a sunbeam.

Try one more thing.

I enjoy being a human, so bottom half dolphin upper half human, with wings, riding to Earth on a sunbeam. Or a dolphin with a human/elf form traveling on a sunbeam, and traveling through the element of water instead of air.

Many beings enjoy this technique today. It is freeing and fun. All of us have shape shifted at will since before time. To understand other species Shapeshifting is fundamental.

Would you say this view debunks humans' superstitions about werewolves and vampires?

Yes, that is the purpose of this lesson---to relieve fear and open the mind to divine love.

I know that in ancient times warriors learned to shape shift by calling upon the powers of their totem animals, and that hunting played an important part in training soldiers from early times to medieval chivalry. To hunt, humans needed to learn to blend into the background and used camouflage to sneak up on their prey. They needed to know the habits of animals and how to be in harmony with the environment. These skills parallel the skills of a Shapeshifter. They are the same skills needed for learning the basics of interspecies communication.

CHAPTER NINE

Dutch's Soul Myth: Horse Pride

It's a warm spring afternoon at the park with the dogs. The sun is shining and it's in the 60s. As I close my eyes to meditate and write my 42-year-old horse's soul myth, I see him jump into the pasture as a baby horse.

I jumped out of my mother and started to run right away. They could hardly contain me. I still feel like jumping sometimes.

I always knew my life had meaning far beyond what the humans knew. They could not see my higher purpose, but I knew it was there. I was flying a long time in the spirit world. I was a horse, a dog, a wild boar, and many times I was a wild animal. I came to Earth because my purpose was to fight for Horse Pride. Horse Pride is melding your purpose so perfectly in union with the higher power that your chest explodes with love and everyone who sees you feels the love that you are. They see the love that you are in your eyes.

"Horse Pride" is the name of my soul's myth. It is the pride I feel in my age, my body, my purpose. There is power in Self Love. I have learned to live from a place of self-empowerment. Self-empowerment is not selfish or self-centered. It is about unity with the grand design, the Great Plan; a deeper, higher purpose that you can only find if you try hard to love yourself.

When I want to reach for the stars, I shine my light out into the night. When I want to reach Ellie, I open my nostrils and allow her fragrance to penetrate my brain. My Horse Pride, wisdom, love, the energy I am made of, is in my deep chest, my strong limbs, my wisdom that comes from my age and my years of experience. My wisdom is waiting to catch up to my purpose.

Our purpose is often just out of our reach and keeps us moving forward. My purpose is to help you move through life with more ease and love. From that place of spiritual exchange I will continue to guide you forward. Communing with me is our form of spiritual exchange.

My soul's purpose is to flow with life. Now that I am stiff and old, my purpose may not be able to continue to grow. It is when that experience peaks that my soul matrix will disintegrate and I will dissolve into my matter-less place. From there, I will regain my flexibility. From there, I will bend my ear and heart toward you and Buddy as your helper and as a bearer of the weight of the work of the translation you are about to make between worlds, human and horse.

I had to wait long for my spiritual fruition. Buddy's soul grew very large, very fast. My soul is about enduring for the long-term, but there are many benefits too.

I want to be remembered for my endurance and as a Gatekeeper for your transition back into Buddy's work for us all. I am a horse from the old school. I rejoice in knowing horses will have a voice in the future with humans. And I rejoice to be allowed to be a part of that work. It keeps me excited about the future. It is just what we (horses) need---a spiritual voice.

Dutch, you are a huge support to all those around you. What spiritual seeds would you like plant for the future?

You look frightened sometimes. I would like to plant a seed that you not be frightened, and that you have the courage to finish your life's work with Buddy. My soul is about enduring to the end.

Yes. Dutch. I will endure as well. This place is my temple. This park bench in the woods. It is here that I feel my spirit soothed, my emotions smoothed, my inner voice heard. I feel in harmony with this place. The sun is shining through the trees, filtering soft shadows onto the ground. The path leads through the woods, and few people pass here. The air is filling with smoke from the campfires below by the river. I hear dogs barking and children playing on the lawn. The stillness feels good. Every so often a crack from a branch or an exploding seed pierces the silence.

The energy of nature heals the human condition. To help preserve it is important. Horses are included in that place of nature. So my soul wishes for the Earth to continue to heal all living creatures. That is the Earth's soul purpose, to heal us. As I process these feelings, the wind blows on my eyelashes. It is cooling. Without wind we may not be able to continue. The Earth has a method to its workings. Living by nature's laws also has been a purpose of mine. Not to go against nature, but to flow with it. My soul is not a myth. My soul is a matrix of experience. I can wander around for days inside these memories. This is a fine day to remember. (As I write this, I can see a constellation of Dutch's past lives and families. He finished by reminding me to write my life story in pencil.

Use only pencils to write your soul myths. Do not make them permanent with permanent ink. We are temporal and impermanent, all.

Dutch died at the age of forty-two on the eve before a Full Grain Moon on August 15, 2008. He was peaceful and full of dignity. He was standing when the vet arrived, the sun was shining, and all were honoring him. After his death I wrote the following:

Dutch is not allowing me to mourn. Whenever I start to feel sad, he just reminds me of his love for me and what happened at the end when I prayed for him. As I meditated on the Tibetan Buddhist Phowa Practice, I saw Christ's presence. Christ had one hand on my shoulder and one hand on Dutch's back. This connection tied us together in love and it was the salve that eased Dutch in the moment of his passing.

Since then, I have not cried. Moving on that day was Dutch's choice. We had several talks about his life and he told me that he was ready to move on. He was suffering from acute kidney failure and in severe pain. He stood for the vet unafraid. No doubts, just love in his heart. His final resting place is under the tall pines behind the barn. No renderer for this boy. He will not be dog food or collagen. All that he is, is still alive in all who knew him. He amazed us with his longevity.

I was scheduled to give a workshop in animal communication the next day after Dutch's passing. When I focused on him that day he came to me and said:

There is only love.

In the Tibetan literature the "Phowa Practice" is a Buddhist meditation that helps a being eject his or her consciousness at the time of death into the world of spirit. As I did this for Dutch that day, I saw him in my mind's eye curl up in a fetal position in Christ's lap. He knew he was loved and he felt deeply cared for. As I finished, I looked at Dutch and his eyes were filled with love. He raised his head wide-eyed, starring into space. I know he felt the powerful message and it soothed him in his final hour.

Section 3

The Mythology of Equus
Part Two : The Horse Goddess

SOFT MOON SHINING

My beloved Divine Mother
Dance with me
under the soft moon shining
in the wide-open fields
far beyond the toil and trouble
of my busy mind
Dance with me
before the night grows old
while the winds of love
still bow the grasses
and the coyotes cry for you
to step their way
Dance with me my beloved
while the Mystery's Edge
still flirts in the shadow
of your radiant light

Soft Moon Shining
Ethan Walker III

CHAPTER TEN

Heaven-Bound on the Wings of a
Dream-Horse

For this section, Ellie has devoted herself to the discovery of God in the feminine form, the Goddess, Divine Mother. Through Ellie's myths we will experience the creatrix of the universe who expresses compassion and love in a direct and intimate way---in the same way that a loving mother would care for her young.

Ellie's myths express the Divine Mother/Goddess who abides in the heart. She is the Goddess who has manifested these forms of consciousness as adoration for Her beloved, the eternal, formless Supreme Being--God the Father.

In truth, these two Gods are not two but one. They are inseparably bound to play out their eternal cosmic dance. The Goddess came from nowhere, meaning that there was never a time when She did not exist. She is that aspect of the divine that is receptive and approachable. Where there is love, compassion and mercy, we can see Her direct presence. She lives in the present moment.

Who is the Goddess?

Mythical tales of ascension on the wings of a horse predate the Bible itself. The first accounts came from the Asiatic Hunters who crossed the Bering Strait some 20,000 years ago. Those immortal, winged-horse riders were the first Shamans of antiquity and their myths of ecstasy and spiritual flight continue to fuel human passion.

Several thousand years later, out of the collective unconscious of classical Greece, another winged-horse myth emerged: Pegasus, the celestial white Moon Horse, conceived of an illicit union between Medusa and the Sea God, Poseidon.

For this chapter, we will discuss Medusa who was originally represented as a powerful natural force and revered by many cultures as sacred and holy. She was a symbol of the full power of the Moon, the Great Triple Goddess. Her images in Old Europe originated thousands of years before her re-invention in classical Greece.

In the Upper Paleolithic, Her powers were expressed through the labyrinth, the uterine image, and various female designs. During the last part of the Stone Age, some 10,000 years ago, Medusa was symbolized by the female figure positioned in holy postures and gestures of empowerment. She was what we might call today, an Animal Communicator because she was often portrayed in the presence of animals, primarily that of birds and snakes, with whom she was intimately connected.

However, when patriarchy took hold during the Bronze and Iron Ages in Greece in the first millennium, the world no longer revered Medusa as born of a sacred mother deity. Instead, they said she was born of a supreme father figure. Because of this shift in thinking, the Earth and Heaven were eternally split. In the new myth, male heroes and gods dominated and subjugated females and all natural forces.

Now, through male domination, the Hero began to conquer the cyclical patterns of nature, making it linear to fit his views. He tamed the wild feminine forces and made women conform to male-servicing gender roles. Soon, the holy image of Medusa, as an ancient symbol of female power and wisdom, was usurped.

By the 6th century B.C., her rites were cut off, her sanctuaries invaded, her sacred groves cut down, her priestesses violated and her images defiled. The meaningful associations (and, by extension, women themselves) were overpowered. The new male order made her into an ugly demon.

Modern Medusa: Path of Initiation

As a modern feminine archetype, Medusa offers women today a path of initiation. She represents the lost underworld queen-- the female incarnation of Pluto. As such, she signifies all the forces of the primordial Great Goddess, with sovereign female wisdom, representing universal creativity and destruction.

She is the Guardian of the Thresholds, Mediatrix between Realms. She is the Mistress of the Beasts who destroys to recreate balance in the world. She represents wholeness behind duality. She controls the untamable and, as a young woman, symbolizes fertility and life itself.

Consequently, the myth of Medusa represents the descent inward into the depths of the psyche, where we all must confront our demons. One by one, we face our repressed fears, hate and anger. Then, through this soul purging, we transform ourselves. At the same time, our phantoms rise to the surface where we can deal with them openly and honestly.

Medusa symbolizes emotional and spiritual transformation. Sometimes transformation appears through the death of a marriage, the loss of a job, a friend or beloved home. The variations are endless. But one way or another, we must give up something we thought we could not live without. Whatever the initial experience of the sacrifice, it sends us spiraling down into the unknown depths where we must face our true selves. As we descend, our treasured belongings, possessions, attitudes and beliefs are stripped away from us. We no longer have a sense of foundation, either emotional or spiritual. At last we reach the bottom where we must come to face what we fear the most. Through this process of initiation (pain, grief and darkness), we finally realize a spiritual rebirth.

CHAPTER ELEVEN

The Goddess and the Horse
A Conversation with Ellie:
Restoring Power to the Goddess

In the following dream-inspired myths we will visit the realms of the lost Moon Goddess to resurrect our own powers of the mystic feminine archetype. In many ways, these myths symbolize a Shamanic soul retrieval for humanity's lost feminine psyche.

This work took me from my first Shamanic initiation in the caves of Southern France to my subsequent awakening with my four-legged myth-weavers, Buddy, Ellie and Dutch. The miracle is not that we are reinventing myths, but that these spiritually minded horses are the living legends of a modern era. They are the master guides and teachers who have returned to Earth to help us rediscover our own lost, mythic roots.

To raise this lost (but not forgotten) power, we will see through new eyes and attune ourselves to new Muses. Raising our Goddess vibration and our Kundalini through inspirational mythic themes, we can rediscover the Winged-Horse behind these mythical masterpieces and reconnect with the One

Conscious Source at the fount of all creation.

Ellie begins the storytelling process while grazing in her summer pasture at our home in Oregon:

Everything is like a woven tapestry. The focus of which is not known for many millennia because we are too close to see it or know it. Yet, when it is almost complete, that is when we can make out its significance. Like an embryo deciding what to become, all is incomprehensible at first. So we wait for first light and first sound, for the tapestry to mature, to ripen. As we do, we are given clues about how to move through it, to add or harmonize with it as we see fit. If we do not wait quietly, our thoughts will trample us. We need to hold small, simple thoughts that cannot hold us captive. We need space and freedom to roam and move about within our thoughts. So, small steps, simple thoughts. Not a herd of thoughts that could create a stampede if we allow them to get the better of us.

We can work with one small bit of material at a time, not all myths at once. That would be too much for any mind to hold or understand. Sink into a single myth at a time with an open mind and open eyes. We can sink into a myth now. Relax and enjoy.

Why is the Goddess so important in human mythology? Does Equine Goddess mythology relate to human Goddess mythology?

All of Equus is from a star system, far, far, from here. Where do you need us today?

I need you here with me on Earth. Since you were bred as a Thoroughbred Racehorse, would you like to talk about "The Goddess and The Racehorse?"

To commune with me you must cut loose. Expand. Open. Feel deeply inside. Feel free inside. The Goddess is not chained or held back in any way. Neither in hate, nor anger, not by any dark forces. The Goddess has a jeweled mind. We come from rubies and emeralds, all glittering with clear color and hard, smooth perfection. You will

143

get there. I am leading you down a path. Open you must, trust you will. Share what you seek, playfully, carefully, joyfully, gently, descending into the mind/mine, from where Goddess energy springs forth.

The Goddess is an energy pattern. We know there are tree goddesses, rock goddesses, and Earth goddesses. It is a type of soul expression that begins slowly, expands, and brings forth fruit of all varieties into intensity. The Goddess in me is deeply encoded to love and be loved. In a bright star-filled sky, look to the stars, move into a star with your open heart. What do you see?

The Goddess works with the senses. The feeling senses, smell, taste, touch and sight. We will work first with the hearing sense. The silence of love is where we come from; out of the deep silence we tone a sound that we love and all the souls that love that sound come to dance around us. Then we display our toned creation for all eyes to see. The tone goes into our eyes where our hearts reflect more to become, our eyes shine out to the stars with the tone, and then there is form. Sound, light, stars and silence. Still, we come from a deep, rich, dark silence. A simple tone created us, and all that we are.

We are the music of stars and planets, the great Void and Beauty. Each star has a sound and if you maintain that sound you will become that sound. Each species has its own tone, its own true Voice, it is the sound of their Soul, and it can be traced into the darkness and the silent universe filled with stardust.

We come from a symphony of stars and stillness. I am manifest from my own star jam. I am Star stuff made into living matter, an Earth-nuclear biostar, matter mixed with clay, Earth with fire, from sun and Earth. I connect at the star level, through my astral intelligence to be perceptible to human eyes in this cosmic garden called Earth. This Earthly garden is made from this "prima materia."

144

I danced for my living, as a star dancer would, bright, shiny, and full of light, sparkling across galaxies until I met with Earth's pull. The Earth's consciousness pulled me and all species of the cosmos to Herself, as she needed. We are only released into the Void again when we are no longer able to maintain our stellar vibration, or when Mother Earth cannot support us any longer. What Earth needs, she puts out to the universe, and the universe feels the attraction and she responds. Every soul, species, human or nonhuman, is an answer to Earth's prayers. Earth is the Mother Goddess of us all. Our species came to the planet Earth because it is where we were called.

Why did Earth call to horses? Why did Earth call on the spirit of Equus?

Earth needed help with Her waters, Her oceans, lakes, rivers and seas. She called to the universe and the soul of the horse responded to that call. After coming from the stars, the spirit and soul of the species Equus went straight into Earth's oceans, and all Her waterways and our vibrations and frequencies changed the Earth's water. Afterwards, the Earth's water was different. Then, Earth called to us again and we came out of Her waters and moved onto Her land.

Why were you called onto the land?

To help the humans move across the surface, to plant seeds and grow in size and number. We are no longer needed for that purpose but humans have fallen in love--which is to say that they recognize our love, the love we are made of, and they have chosen to keep us here. Many of our species returned home as their jobs were finished. But those of us who chose to stay did so for the love of humanity.

Ellie, sensing my deeper emotions, continued:

Yes. That shocks you, but it is true. We love you more than you love yourselves, obviously, or you would not be so shocked to hear me say this.

Well, it seems humanity has abused the love that horses have for us. Maybe my guilt chokes the feeling of love in me.

Yes. That is why you would like to have us stay. It is because we love you, feel your pain, and would like to help you clear yourselves of the terrible ignorance that breeds your fear.

How do you do that?

By loving you when you least expect it. We know we can go home anytime. All our families are waiting for us, watching us suffering at the hand of humans, hoping we are doing the right thing by staying to help you. Someday those who left may all be called back to Earth again. Earth is a heavenly home until she no longer can support her children and sustain them. All beings answer the call, the dream of Earth. We respond to Her desires, and she mothers us well. We often wish to return just to experience her beauty again. We, the Goddess of the Horse, are a sacred part of that immeasurable beauty. We make Earth more beautiful with our presence. But we know we are made of star stuff and clay and we may all be called home anytime, which is our true dimension.

What are your brothers and sisters doing now, those who left Earth? Are they waiting to return here?

They see us. They know of our suffering and they help us whenever they can. All we need to do is remember who we truly are, and where we truly come from and we can awaken them, and they do awaken in us, and we are all saved by this re-membering. We are not so lonely then, when we re-member and feel our star stuff, which is light and sparkling and shining, and reflective like crystals, and we don't feel heavy, which is more of an Earthly joy. Earth love is heavier. So those of you who have forgotten where you come from, you feel much heavier. If you cannot lighten up, remember that you are made of the same star stuff as we are.

Earth called humans too. If She decides that She no longer needs you, She may release you back to your heavenly home. But, just as you kept horses because you loved them, not because of their original star purpose, but because you were learning from them about love, Earth may decide She loves you too, beyond your original star purpose, and She may allow you to stay here as well. There are those who may not wish to stay, since everyone chooses in life. However, when we leave, it is because there is a strong universal pull to leave, unless we really try hard to change Her wishes. You and we all have the freedom to choose where we go next in our evolutionary journey. How long we stay and when and if we return is our choice.

Why did Mother Earth call humans to Her?

Humans were called to become broadcast stations, as a part of a large communication grid between galaxies. The purpose of humanity on Earth is to radiate, beam, send, transmit, or channel the power of the Earth out into the Universe to see if other Universes respond. It is Her way of communicating and sharing knowledge with other galaxies and star systems, through human transponders. It is Earth's way of reaching into the Void to communicate. We could all grow and expand if we pooled our universal resources.

Has humanity aided in finding new resources, to further evolution on Earth?

Yes. You have become more fruitful in that regard. You still have a lot to learn about interpreting frequencies and vibrations coming into Earth's atmosphere, and about sharing this among yourselves. One day, as in the past, you will learn how to mitigate the many atrocities you have committed against your Mother. You will learn this through cooperation and sharing with each other. Someone will discover the information needed: The more you search for it, the more it will be shown to you.

Are we achieving our goals for Earth?
Yes. Now take a deep breath, sit back and relax.

Put away all hindrances. Let your mind, full of love, pervade
The whole wide world
Above, below, around, and everywhere,
Altogether continue to pervade with love-filled thoughts,
Abounding, sublime, beyond measure.
~ The Buddha

Ellie and our new horse Ro

CHAPTER TWELVE

Myth of the Goddess and the Horse

In the mountain hermitage which is my body,
In the temple of my breast,
At the summit of the triangle of my heart,
The horse, which is my mind, flies like the wind.
He gallops on the plains of great bliss.
If he persists, he will attain the rank of a victorious Buddha.
Going backward, he cuts the root of samsara;
Going forward he reaches the high land of Buddhahood.
Astride such a horse, one attains the highest illumination.
~ The 100,000 Songs of Milarepa
Translation by Losang P. Lhalungpa

Now that we can appreciate the essence of the Goddess, and how her energy has been suppressed for so many centuries, let us turn to Ellie's soul myth, *The Goddess and the Horse.*

To appreciate myths to their fullest, readers must remember that myths are written using symbols, and symbols are not to be taken literally, but rather as metaphors. This concept requires us to go with the flow of the material, to be open to our deeper feelings and inner awareness.

As I begin to meditate with Ellie to transcribe her myth, I feel how peaceful she is standing next to Buddy in the pasture. When our communications begin, often whole scenes unfold as I write the words that come by way of articulating them. Words and phrases come on their own, and then more images follow. This process builds upon itself the more I relax into the meditation.

It feels right to want to awaken the Goddess of All Life in these times of war. The Goddess is not a warring deity. She is about compassion and that is how she rules.

Ellie, there is a need for humans to know more compassion. Can you show this by telling a myth about The Goddess and the Horse?

Yes. Give me a moment to immerse myself in those memories and feelings.

The world is clean and fresh. It smells like new mown grass, all green and lush with morning dew. I see my reflection in each dewdrop as I eat grass here. If you come closer, you too will see your reflection.

As we enter the dewdrop portal, we are transported down a spiraling tunnel, deep into the bowels of Earth. Round and round we fall deeper and deeper, until we reach a verdant meadow where we see several white unicorns grazing quietly together. A soft, pale light drapes the creatures in the stillness of dawn. Some unicorns have red horns; some blue, others yellow and green. Pick one to walk beside.

I choose the Blue Horned Unicorn, wondering if she will let us follow her. Her pure white fur surrounds her sapphire eyes, set in radiant gold and blue. She smiles and our hearts open wide.

"Can we follow you?" I ask, feeling awkward in the presence of such an ethereal being. The Unicorn looks up and says:

"Welcome. You may enter here. I am the Gatekeeper. But you will pass many gates before you meet the Goddess that you seek. Before you pass through my gate you must divest yourselves of something you hold dear. You may think for a moment before deciding."

Ellie thinks for a moment. *I love my tail, jet black, all lustrous, shining and thick. It has always been my crowning glory, flowing freely as I run against the wind.*

Ellie decides to let go of her tail and instantly it falls to the ground. It is as though she had placed it there carefully, with pride. I close my eyes and agree to let go of the first thing that comes to mind. Immediately, I know it is my right foot. I check again. My right foot is symbolic of my foundation in the material world, my anchor in three-dimensional reality. How can I walk on only one foot? But I am beginning to trust the process and off goes my right foot! As it does, I see it fall next to Ellie's tail. We look at the Blue Horned Unicorn for approval. The Blue Horned Unicorn smiles and says, "Come this way."

Following behind the Blue Horned Unicorn, I realize I can walk on only one foot, using my mind for balance. Ahead we see two glistening white marble columns. At first they appear as ice columns, yet, when we get closer we feel they are warm and smooth. "Where are we?" I ask.

The Blue Horned Unicorn replies, "We are in the waiting room where traveling souls prepare for the next step on their journey. Now, you both must give up all of your physical attributes, your clothing and bodies alike."

As we begin to let go completely, we find ourselves immediately draped in fine silk robes. Ellie's garment covers her whole body, while mine is much smaller and seems not to fit me as well. I can see through it so that makes me feel better. Then, our robes start swirling around the room, taking on flowing shapes. Gradually, we find ourselves floating effortlessly across the marble floor with our flowing robes.

"These are the Mansions of the Mind of the Goddess," the Blue Unicorn tells us. "Take a moment to enjoy the awe that she inspires."

I sense her pristine purity cleansing our negative thoughts and feelings. Everything of the past fades into the background and I realize we are far away from home.

My silk robe begins to sway as though it wants me to dance with it. I feel the Robe has a life force of its own. I go with it across the floor, but suddenly find myself prostrating on the floor. Then I see Ellie floating above me on the ceiling. Her robe has taken her flying higher. I hear Ellie's laughter and joyfulness as she floats overhead.

Now the Blue Horned Unicorn calls to her friends and instantly the Red, Yellow, and Green Horned Unicorns appear in the room. The Blue Horned Unicorn tells us, "I will leave you now. But, choose well your guides from here." Then the Unicorns leave.

By the seriousness of the Blue Unicorn's tone we take her message as a warning. I move closer to Ellie and ask what she wants to do.

Follow me.

Then, as we are about to leave, we hear another disembodied feminine voice speaking to us from above us.

152

"I am the Goddess of the Moon," the voice says softly. "You are inside my mind now. From here you will speak with me directly. What is it that you seek?"

Abruptly, we find ourselves inside a marble temple chamber with the Goddess of the Moon. There is a great crackling sound at the center of the room as the marble floor opens with a heavy, trembling thrust. Up from the floor comes a huge blazing hearth. The fire is so hot that it is almost impossible to bear.

We hear the voice of the Goddess speaking again: "Enter here with me."

I am reminded of the warning the Blue Horned Unicorn gave us and ask Ellie how she feels about going into a blazing hot fire. Ellie reminds me our mission is to invoke the Goddess of the Horse. So off into the blaze we go.

The fire begins to work its magic on us, purging and purifying us. When we are finished, we realize we have been transformed into beautiful, white porcelain dolls dressed in white silk robes. Ellie looks at me. I look at her, amazed.

The Goddess of the Moon then appears to us as a glowing orb of white light. She invites us to follow her through the opening in the ceiling that reveals a night sky filled with stars. The shining stars and moonlight from the Goddess shimmer above us as if to hypnotize. Faint bird songs echo in the distance. The Goddess of the Moon speaks as we fly into the sky.

"Why have you come so far? What do you seek?"

I tell her we would like to invoke the Goddess of the Horse.

"I am the Goddess of the Stars and Moon," she responds. "I created the Goddess of the Horse. I am the Keeper of the Key to her Chambers."

Silently we follow the Moon Goddess's voice as we soar upward, our robes trailing behind us like comet tails. Traveling quickly into the shadows, we are trying hard to keep up pace.

In the blink of an eye, we find ourselves standing at the edge of a crystal clear lake. Hundreds of horses, of all different colors, are standing around the edge. The horses are bent over drinking from the still, clear water.

Next, we fly to the center of the lake, looking out at the horses around us in a circle. Overlaying the lake is something that looks like the spokes of a wheel. My head starts to spin as Ellie suddenly dives into the center of the lake, creating a splash. When she emerges again my spinning stops. Now, I am face to face with a beautiful white mare, only this mare is larger and more beautiful than any I have ever seen.

I am the embodiment of the Goddess now. I hear Ellie say in her own voice. *I am inside her looking out at you. Can you see the power of love in my eyes?*

The lake ripples softly back and forth. I struggle to keep my balance.

"Is that you, Ellie? Have we arrived at the Goddess of the Horse?"

Ellie begins to tell the story of the Goddess of the Horse:

Yes. Let us begin the teaching of the 'Good Way of the Horse.' The quiet, steady gallop of the Goddess is in her rhythm, in her graceful movement. As she covers ground, she travels fast, spreading out, expanding, and reaching far. She opens to humans as she answers your deepest questions. She does not react at all. You must sit with her and be calm. Breathe in and listen to her breathing. Do not stir. Close your eyes and open your heart.

"How we can we work with you," I ask, hoping Ellie, now Goddess, is listening to me.

Simple steps are what you seek, but there are many dimensions to explore. The Goddess of the Horse is in her motion, in her stride and how she moves. She has magnificent action, free flowing and soft. She glides with supple beauty. The small of the back is where the ride begins. This is where the Goddess lives in you. In horses too. How you sit on a horse determines what happens to you both. You must sit as though you are deeply in touch with the Goddess. The Goddess in me meets the God/Goddess in you, at the level of our spines.

I have a flexible spine. You have loose limbs, comfortable hands and soft eyes. How does your neck feel when your back is touching the Horse Goddess? Feel your neck and shoulders now. Are they soft and round? Do you find straining in your body at all? This is 'The Yoga of the Goddess of the Horse.' Feel it and remember. You can worship this Goddess completely, with your whole mind and heart, with the small of your back, deep inside your spine.

The Flower of the Goddess opens in the spine. The Lotus Flower is opening inside your heart too. It is a feeling of freedom, flying and floating with joyfulness. The body is free. Your feet touch me lightly, like water rippling at the edge of a lake. So, too, you must make small ripples of energy as you ride, as though you are submerged in water---fluid and light.

The Lotus of the Spine is many-petaled and it supports the whole body. Let go. Feel it. Move into this flowering. Smile, Breathe.

My breath is your breath. I offer you my many winds.

If you are ready, we can take a jump. First, we must balance our winds together, or we may fall. So, touch me lightly and advance. I will follow you. Slowly, and then, more quickly. Do not let go of your Lotus Seat on my Lotus Spine. Elevate yourself to the marble mansions of the mind of the Goddess. Let us find an obstacle to navigate.

I see a stream, a fallen tree, a rock.

No problem. Hold on gently.

The wind blows through my hair and across my face as we begin soaring over the stream with wings of spirit that lift us up and back down again. The Earth rises softly to meet us like a ribbon of silk. We take the next jump. Again, Ellie flies over each with grace and ease.

These feelings evoke a thrill of adventure that I love, but I cannot hold on any longer and I plummet back to Earth, into my body again, and open my eyes. At home, I remember the freedom and joy horseback riding brings, and how this ecstatic feeling feeds the soul.

Ellie

CHAPTER THIRTEEN

Commentary: Cultivating
Understanding of Myth and Metaphor

In order to cultivate a deeper understanding of the symbols Ellie used to tell her myth, and to realize the capacity they have to transform us, we will focus on the symbols to provide a greater awareness of how mythology exerts its influence on the subconscious mind.

"The world is new and fresh . . ." Ellie sets the stage while observing her reflection in a morning dewdrop. Her nose is pressed to the ground as she grazes on lush, green grass. The use of the metaphor, "morning dew," is a lovely beginning for this myth. According to Emanuel Swedenborg, a noted 16th century Swedish philosopher, the symbolic significance of morning dew is the truth of peace. In his book "Divine Providence," he notes, "Dew signifies the truth of peace because in the morning, dew comes down from the heavens and appears upon the grass like fine rain. Also, it has stored in it something of the sweetness or delight of heaven, more so than rain itself. Dew gladdens the grass and the crops of the field."

He further explains, "Morning also denotes a state of peace. Peace implies a new dawn on the Earth, making minds and hearts happy with universal delight. The truth of peace is the light of dawn that affects all things and makes heaven, heaven. Peace has the confidence of the Lord in it that touches all things and provides for all things, and leads to a good end. In a genuine sense, dew is the truth of good that comes from a state of innocence."

Our myth gives birth to a great deal more in a spiritual sense than objective reality or literal meaning. It implies an entrance into a divine state of consciousness, which is how transformation takes place.

Next, we enter the "dew drop portal," moving down through a "spiraling tunnel," deep into the bowels of the Earth. The spiraling tunnel is a metaphor for the universal, archetypal symbol of the spiritual path, as depicted on the cave walls and on clay pots thousands of years ago by our ancestors. It draws our attention to the unfolding path of evolution while symbolizing the divine potential of all beings on the long and winding road of life.

In its highest aspect, the spiral refers to the movement of Kundalini energy---a Sanskrit term meaning "spiral" or "circular." The Kundalini energy connects us to our creative center or divine oneness. Kundalini is the etheric counterpart of the spinal column. It is said that we arouse Kundalini when we act out of divine love and compassion for others and ourselves. This energy lays dormant at the base of the spine until it is activated, as in the practice of Yoga. It is channeled upward through the body's energy centers/Chakras, in the process of spiritual enlightenment.

For a person whose Kundalini remains asleep at the base of the spine, he or she lives in the empirical world with little access to the power that those who have awakened their Kundalini find in the subtle, spiritual dimensions. The spiral movement of Kundalini typifies the movement of the Chakras. The Chakras hold the spiritual energy that animates the physical body. The tunnel in our myth metaphorically joins our consciousness as a point of entry to these higher dimensions. A tunnel goes below the Earth while a bridge goes above it. In Shamanic terms, a tunnel or a hole in the Earth is how Shamans journey into nonordinary reality . . . the realm of the spirit.

During a Shamanic Journey the Shaman joins with one or more power animals at the end of a long tunnel. These power animals are aspects of the higher self that can provide guidance, knowledge and healing. Alternatively, these animals may help the Shaman travel onward to other spiritual dimensions where he or she meets additional guides or other spirit animals.

As the tunnel symbolizes the shape of a Chakra the spiral signifies its movement. So it can be said that we have embarked on a journey down through a spiraling Chakra (vortex) and portal into another dimension. In addition, the tunnel may also signify the birthing canal, a place subconsciously known as the passageway to liberation, as in the phrase, "the light at the end of the tunnel."

Simply said, Chakras are energy vortexes that animate the body physically. The Chakra does not originate inside the body, as some believe. Instead, it animates the body from the macrocosm to the microcosm. These vortexes are connected to the body, via invisible subtle passageways up and down the spinal column called Nadis.

Chakras spiritually animate animals, as well as people, plants and the environment. Chakras create what is called the "aura." All life forms have an aura that anyone sensitive enough can see and feel. As our myth continues, we reach a meadow at the end of the tunnel, where we encounter various unicorns grazing quietly. A unicorn is an ancient mythological creature that enjoys a rich and complex history. All over the world, the belief in the existence of unicorns has endured longer than any other mythical animal, well into the 19th century. Some accounts date back to the time of Atlantis when it is said that unicorns perished in the Great Flood.

Every society has developed their own version of this mythological creature, as seen through different cultural lenses. In early Christianity, the unicorn symbolized the purity of Christ and could only be captured or successfully hunted by a virgin. It is, as such, indicative of the Virgin Mary. It is believed that unicorns represent human desire to be closer to God by working toward greater clarity and virtue.

Mythologists tell us that unicorns symbolize the principle that unites the spectrum of color, either white or multicolored. In its white, ethereal light body, a unicorn contains all the colors of the rainbow. The one color is the essence of the multi-colored. If one is pure in heart, a unicorn will appear in its visible, white form. In Greco-Roman lore, a unicorn is an attribute of the Virgin Moon Goddesses, Artemis, whose chariot is drawn by eight unicorns. The Virgin Moon Goddess is also mentioned later in our myth.

Unicorns represent gentleness, chastity, and strength of mind. Thus, the unicorn is associated with royalty, as the single horn is an emblem of unlimited and individual power.

Buddy on Unicorns with Dawn Baumann Brunke

In the following telepathic conversation between Dawn Baumann Brunke, author of *Animal Voices: Telepathic*

160

Communication in the Web of Life, and Buddy, Buddy reveals a deeper, mythological meaning for unicorns in human culture.

The unicorn reveals and illustrates a point of connection between this mythic animal and human beings. Here we come to the intersection of several different layers of reality—including several layers of Earth reality, legend, and psychic reality.

Buddy shows this information visually as flipping through the pages in a book, the idea that all are a part of the story. However, if you look at one page, you are in one time, and if you look at another, you are in another time. Yet, all are connected or held within a particular focus of the book.

Let us begin with the mythic aspect of the unicorn. You might begin by asking why UNI-corn, why one horn, and remember that a horn is different from an antler. The unicorn's horn is an outgrowth; it relates to an exaggeration of the third eye and is a touchstone to this connection, as in a memory. There are several threads to follow. We will pull it in as an aspect of how myths are "mirrored" between humans and animals, and legendary animals as well.

The unicorn is a real animal in the sense that it arose from the primal connections between humans, animals and the Earth. It is important to see this triad in understanding the unicorn story. The unicorn is actually about three, and the connection between the triad.

That the unicorn is considered legendary is an indication of how this connection between man, animal and land is perceived--it too is legendary. (As an aside, an underlying pattern of "lost mythical creatures" is nearly always a psychic yearning to re-find the lost connection--an attempt to thread one's way back to the primary connection between humans, animals and nature/land). That is another discussion, but one that fits within the larger mythic framework.

The "lost connection" between humans and unicorns is on

one level about loss of innocence, loss of connection with the divine within the animal kingdom. See it like this: Animals hold a connection to the Earth and move in concert with their viewpoint of the land, water and air. Each has its own job as well as positive and negative aspects to help balance the Earth and all of creation. When one species becomes extinct, there is a "hole" in the fabric or web, and this hole needs to be filled, either by another species or as with the unicorn, by an energetic hold; in this instance, the 'memory' of a legendary/mythical creature. This is a key to remembering and accessing the energy once held by unicorns and the connection between them, the Earth and us.

Are unicorns a part of the horse tribe?

Yes. Though not in the way commonly assumed. They are not a 'lost' tribe (species) of horse; rather, they are the representation of a specific energetic connection between horses (and some other animals) and humans. The unicorn holds the psychic third eye connection. Some horses hold this energetic as well--if you feel slightly above the forehead of some horses, you will notice a hump or elevation of this energy above and between the eyes. This also is a holding, a memory of the psychic connection between humans and horses.

The centaur (horse/man) connection is similar, but more founded on the physical union of horses and humans--not in a sexual manner but derived of the closeness between the two, depicted in riding--when humans could 'ride the consciousness' of horses or other animals so well they merged. It too is a vision of a forgotten connection. Do you understand how these images hold certain memories?

I do. What I get is that the question is not so much—whether these beings are "real," but rather, how we re-merge with these models of energy to understand and re-member these forgotten pieces of our dynamic connection.

162

That is exactly it. In the same way, myths or legends hold a piece of remembering for you, the energy is couched within the story. It is up to you to enter with a specific focus of consciousness, a certain vibration or frequency or attunement to the story--and it is this attunement that "unlocks' the myth or legend and allows you to enter the energy under the story, the energy held within the story.

So the story, myth, or legend is a vehicle.

Exactly. Myths are 'fanciful' vehicles through which a more direct experience of energy underlying the surface reality is apprehended, experienced and known. These are the "human digging days"--to recall these songs, legends, myths and stories, not just for the purpose of retelling or collecting them, but to use them as doorways, as portals. Human consciousness as a whole--this is your story--going out into the world, leaving your connections, having many experiences, and then returning to re-find all that you knew and know again but in another context.

Digest this for now. This is a tremendous undertaking. We are simply sketching the surface. It is just enough for readers to move with it. It is as if we are giving you 'how to' instructions for the beginning of the treasure hunt, for you to take these tools and begin the process of reclaiming yourselves and your energies by putting the pieces of the puzzle together.

As we begin to participate more and more in cosmic co-creation with nonhuman species, we will understand the process of Mythmaking that Buddy is talking about with Dawn in the above dialogue. For now, we continue to interpret Ellie's myth of The Goddess and the Horse.

We are aware of many different colored unicorns' horns; red, yellow, orange, green and blue. These declare the presence of a spiritual power that is inherent in each of the Chakra centers. The White Horned Unicorn represents unity of soul with the divine through the combined essence of the other

Chakras. Its presence suggests that our myth is working at a deeper level of unity through the physical body and the senses. Ellie is manifesting healing through the speech center, the Fifth Chakra, and the written word. She is also connecting us to love through the fourth or Heart Chakra. In addition, because the unicorn relates to the Sixth Chakra, the third eye center is being activated. Thus, healing occurs on a deep, psychic level through higher awareness and insight.

The Chakras exist in many dimensions simultaneously. As such, they become our point of entry into other realities.

The Blue Horned Unicorn, (communication center) welcomes us, and reminds us that we have many gates through which we must pass before meeting the Goddess. These gates are metaphors or psychic counterparts for the five senses, the centers we must work with to purify and balance before we can move forward on our journey toward enlightenment.

Then the Gatekeeper or Portal Guardian, the Blue Horned Unicorn, asks us to divest or dispossess ourselves of something we hold dear. The Portal guardian represents the boundary between our conscious and unconscious minds. The Guardian protects us from becoming overwhelmed by all of our memories at once, by all the archetypes and the collective unconscious itself. The Gatekeeper decides what memories are allowed to come to the surface. Some truth-seekers must learn to love the Gatekeeper unconditionally before they can access the divine mind.

Our sacrifices suggest that we need to extract the essence of the soul and relinquish those things we no longer need in the physical world. We do this to unite sides, dark and light, yin and yang, male and female. Perhaps it illustrates releasing negative mental conditioning, bad habits, addictions and/or unhealthy dependencies. The Guardian asks us to think before we decide what to give up, so that we may move forward our path of discovery. What happens next is a universal and natural process.

Those raised in Western culture may relate to it more than others. It is interesting Ellie and I renounce the same thing symbolically. That is, we decide to relinquish our 'foothold' and 'tailhold' in the material world. These are our physical and psychological connections to third dimensional reality. Her tail and my right foot represent our Earthly ties to worldly concerns. They represent those thoughts and emotions that motivate us to invest our cherished and limited time on the Earth, our energy and resources, to acquire material things so that we can provide proof of our worthiness to others and to ourselves.

In other words, for me, it is my attachment to material things. It is why many work--not only for food, shelter and clothing--but for big houses, luxury cars, far-off vacations, expensive boats, etc. For Ellie, it is her attachment to her own Earthly pleasures, to her senses and feeling the wind.

Letting go of the myth of the Self in this way supports our higher purpose and sense of spirituality. According to the sages of old, we cannot enter heaven without renouncing the things of this world. Therefore, it is fitting that we give up the things that represent our attachment to materialism. Relinquishing these connections suits our goal which is to merge with the Goddess.

"Come this way," the Goddess tells us. As we agree, we see two glistening columns of white marble across the horizon. The esoteric significance of marble is that it gives an intellectual connection to ancient civilizations. In healing, it is used for clarity in meditative states, and it promotes peak states of awareness with total recall in dreams. It provides guidance in the purification and control of our thoughts and can help us to manifest our desires.

The twin columns represent wisdom. They are also symbolic of the link between heaven and Earth. In a building, columns support the structure and stand for stability. Therefore, with marble columns we have a reference to the heavenly, healing support of ancient wisdom, as we experience assistance in achieving our goals through meditative states of consciousness.

Moving along, we are asked to give up all our physical attributes--our clothes and physical bodies alike. When we consent, we are immediately draped in white garments, which in the Christian faith are worn by those being baptized. After baptism, wearing white is symbolic of the innocence of the soul. White garments represent purity and glory. Jesus appeared in white when His majesty was revealed on the mountain. As he prayed, the appearance of His face altered and His robe turned glistening white.

Angels also wear white robes. Rev 19:14 "And the armies in heaven, clothed in fine linen, white and clean, followed him on white horses." To take away our worldly garments and replace our bodies with white garments implies that our iniquities are being purified through faith.

Rites of passage are the rituals that prepare us for other-realm sojourns. These rituals are performed when a mortal greets the divine and the divine greets the mortal passing into the realm of the immortal. Eventually they become immortal as well. In the symbolic language of early mystical literature the "garment of glory" or the "garment of light" represents the higher celestial, angelic spiritual nature.

Next, my white garment takes me prostrating on the floor. What is the meaning of prostration? First, we should know why we do not do prostrations. We do not do them to endear ourselves to others. Those who do prostrations do them for the Buddha. They bow to purify their past where they did not show respect for others. Prostrations help humans to realize there is something more meaningful than ourselves. In this way, we purify the pride that we have accumulated through countless lifetimes.

Next, I see Ellie floating on the ceiling. No prostrations for this spirited horse! Floating on the ceiling has a symbolic purpose and points to the idea that in her next life she will actually become a Goddess or a deity of some high position. That is, the nearness to the ceiling refers to her proximity to heaven, to the Gods/Goddesses. She is on her way to becoming a 'heavenly body.'

This is not to be confused with an out-of-body experience, in which we feel we have left the body and can look down at it from above. Floating on the ceiling is a metaphor for being "above it all." I realize from this that I am in good company with Ellie as I see her above me. I know she is already almost a Goddess on Earth and wonder how many horses can be deified in this way.

Next, a bodiless joy fills our hearts. This does refer to the feeling of astral travel in an altered state of consciousness, which is similar to an out-of-body experience. In simple terms, it can be explained as releasing the soul from the ties that bind it to earthly cares for a short time, but remaining connected by way of an etheric cord.

As humans, we typically choose to experience life rather than watch it pass by. By learning to balance these experiences of other dimensions with ordinary reality, we can expand our creative range and extend our spiritual perceptions.

In ordinary reality, we feed this awareness with our

five senses. The intellect takes what comes in through these five gates, organizes it, and creates reality from there. While this reality is also "real," there are many other dimensions and realities to explore that exist simultaneously. Myths take us into some of these "other" realities, and are the means by which we experience them. When we participate in creating our own mythology, we establish our individuality and can express it co-creatively and constructively with others. Myths are just one of the many bridges between worlds.

According to Sam Keen, author of Your *Mythic Journey: Finding Meaning in Your Life Through Writing and Storytelling,* "We are all living stories that have been handed down to us from birth, from our parents, society and nation. If we do not examine these stories to know if they are still relevant and meaningful, we may end up missing the whole point of our lives."

Keen suggests that storytelling is a communal act, that by sharing stories with each other we experience each other's realities. He says to be fully alive we need to answer life's deeper questions for ourselves. Some of these are, "Who am I? Where am I going? Where do I come from? And, what happens when I die?"

Keen tells us that we cannot take these life-changing questions for granted. The myths we have been told by the media, movies, books and religion, ad infinitum no longer hold true for us today. Were they ever true? Can they still guide us? Or, do we need new stories? To live fully is to have a story to tell.

As we move forward, we turn our attention to a crackling fire burning in a great hearth. This hearth is at the center of a secret chamber. In initiation rites, it was common to confine initiates in a secret room, chamber, or cave that

168

represented the womb or the grave. The secret chamber concealed forbidden knowledge that cannot be entered into without pain of penalty. The chamber and fire are also symbolic of a "hermetic" laboratory—a reverberating furnace of the soul. Some version of a furnace always plays a part for the chemist and alchemist alike.

In the book, *Spiritual Alchemy*, C.C. Zain writes, "The furnace of the spiritual alchemist is fed by an outpouring of love. Nothing raises the vibrations as quickly as love. Love operates on various planes, but only unselfish love affects spiritual substance."

The reference to the fire in the hearth points to the alchemical fire used to transform base metals into gold during the Middle Ages. Symbolically, this alchemy is the mystical art for the transformation of the human spirit.

The symbolism of the hearth is that it provides access to the spirits of ancestors dwelling in other worlds. The hearth fire in ancient Greece was the symbol of the religious center of the family.

So off we go into the alchemical fires of purification. When we return, we fly up through the center of the chamber into the night sky. If the Chakra system is balanced and the crown is open and connected to divine guidance, we can travel safely with the third eye, using psychic insight. As we gaze at the sky, we hear another voice. It is the voice of the Goddess of the Moon.

She represents the Great Mother. The Goddess of the Moon is the fertile matrix, out of which all life is born and into which all life is reabsorbed. The Moon rules side-by-side with the Sun God. In some ancient societies, the Moon Goddess was even more important because she bestowed her wisdom and spiritual knowledge onto her people. The night sky refers to being inside the womb of the Goddess of the Moon.

In the next moment, we at the center of a clear lake. Nearly all myths equate water with purity and fertility, as the source of all life. A clear lake implies an emphasis on purity. Without water, there is no life. Here water is not an image or a simile, but a symbol for life itself. It is a symbol of the potential of the formless state of all living things, the precondition of life in its original expression.

In terms of the psyche, water illustrates the feminine unconscious. Water moistens the desert realm of the Ego. It brings life to it. In legend and folklore, a lake is a two-way mirror dividing the natural and the supernatural worlds. A lake is reflective on its smooth surface, which signifies contemplation from above, and observation from below. The transparency of still water symbolizes contemplative perception.

Surrounding our mythic lake, we see horses of all colors. The lake represents a pool of universal knowledge, with the horses all around, seeking knowledge and communication amongst them. Suddenly, we see the spokes of a wheel overlaying the lake.

 The wheel is an ancient symbol of creation, sovereignty and protection. It represents change and motion. In Buddhism, the wheel was adopted as a symbol of the Buddha's teachings, being identical to the wheel of law. In Tibetan culture it means "wheel of transformation" or spiritual change, and can mark the overcoming of all obstacles and illusions.

The spinning Chakras that control the flow of spiritual

energy into matter are often displayed as lotus wheels. The spokes or petals of the heart lotus flower are parts of the pattern that represent different stages of life between birth and death. Here on the clear lake the wheel symbolizes the eight-spoked/petaled wheel or flower of the Heart Chakra. It can also refer to the chariot wheel of ancient times that relates closely to horses. The overlaying wheel has a spiritual meaning, symbolizing the teaching that life has no beginning and no end, and is simultaneously in motion while also at rest.

My head starts to spin as Ellie dives into the center of the lake. The metaphor of "jumping into the lake," symbolizes a concept once introduced by Carl Jung, called enantiodromia. This characteristic phenomenon practically always occurs when an extreme, one-sided tendency dominates the conscious life; and in time an equally powerful counter point is built up, that at first inhibits the consciousness, but then subsequently breaks through our conscious control.

In this case, Ellie makes an immediate switch from her mind to her body. The shock to the body resolves the enigma of the mind. Why does this occur? Because jumping into the water releases the instincts---the instincts swiftly rise to the surface to become the body's light. For an intuitive, the question can often be answered by the instincts.

To plunge into the cold water after the heat of reflection is putting the question into the realm of the instincts, where it ceases to be rigid and begins to flow, as if the answer can be found in the depths of the waters of the unconscious. This metaphor refers to the Chinese concept of yin and yang.

When Ellie emerges, my spinning stops and I am face-to-face with a feminine, spotless white horse.

She says: *I have manifested the Goddess. I am inside of her looking out at you now. Can you see the power of love in her eyes?*

The lake begins to ripple back and forth, and I struggle to stay alert. "Is that you, Ellie?" I ask. "Have you made it into the Heart of the Goddess?" Ellie says:

Yes. Let us begin the teaching of the 'Good Way of the Horse.' The quiet, steady gallop of the Goddess is in Her rhythm, Her movement. She covers ground, traveling widely, spreading out, expanding, reaching far. Opening to humans, she feels the answers to our deepest emotions. Simple steps are what you seek, but there are many dimensions to explore.

I ask about the Goddess and the Horse and Ellie begins with spiritual wisdom expressed through symbolism and imagery from ancient India.

She tells me to imagine a *Flower of the Goddess* opening inside my spine as a visualization for horseback riding. Here the meaning of the flower again has spiritual significance. In early Hindu myths, Brahma and Buddha are shown emerging from flowers. Flowers appear in art as attributes of hope and a new dawn. The colors, scents and qualities of flowers determine their character. The lotus is the most ancient and prolific symbol in the traditions of Egypt, India, China and Japan. What does this flower mean?

 In Buddhism, the lotus is a symbol of purity because it grows out of the mud. Yet it is untarnished by the mud as it reaches toward the light. This is only a superficial explanation. The true lotus is the inner fire inside one's body. The shape of this inner flame resembles a flower. Just as a modern elevator travels up and down, this inner fire blossom ascends and descends inside the body. When it rises to the heart, it transforms the heart into an eight-petaled lotus.

The eight-petaled lotus is the true lotus, which one

obtains through spiritual cultivation. The unenlightened human heart is actually a lotus in an unopened floret. Only when we kindle the inner fire and raise it to the level of the heart is the unopened lotus transformed into an opened, eight-petaled lotus flower.

The Hindus believe that the most mysterious place in the human body is between the cerebrum and the cerebellum. It is shaped like a thousand-petaled lotus. When the inner fire rises, reaching the brow and crown, the thousand-petaled lotus flares, and the fluid stored inside the thousand-petaled lotus flows downward. When the descending fluid (bindu) and the ascending inner fire meet and merge at the heart center, we are transformed into a lotus with the heart as its petals. Buddhists describe this in Tantra as "inner fire ascending, heavenly nectar descending." When these two join in union at the heart, the lotus blooms, and one attains enlightenment.

So, we have come full-circle. The metaphor for *entering the dew drop portal* in the beginning of Ellie's myth brings us back to the purpose and deeper meaning of her story---to enter into a relationship with the vital essence of our own inner, psychic energy, through which we achieve spiritual renewal and ultimately our own divinity.

After much reflection I realized The Goddess and the Horse myth is a reflection of my soul myth wherein the imagery Ellie reveals, as a horse, brings to the surface that which is hidden and asleep in my own unconscious, i.e., the Mother Goddess or Kundalini. Ellie represents herself to me as a Horse Goddess as she takes me through the process of transcending my own darkness (feminine soul) bringing me into the light and my own Self-realization. Readers may experience a similar profound revelation when writing a soul myth with a beloved animal.

In many cultures around the world people believe the crescent form of a horse shoe is linked to the symbol of the Moon Goddess of ancient Europe. The protection invoked is of the Goddess. Some believe the horse shoe must face upward so that their luck will not run out. In other regions they hang the horse shoe pointing downward so their luck can pour in.

Finally, Ellie offers her "many winds" as I ride her lotus spine. What does she mean by her many winds and her lotus spine? To understand the meaning of the symbolism, we will turn to the next chapter titled *Channels, Winds & Essences*.

CHAPTER FOURTEEN

Channels, Winds & Essences

'White Wind is the galactic wind, the catalyzing current, the Spirit that moves through all things. It is the divine breath that gives life to all creation, the unseen essence of solar energy. White Wind is the breath of inspiration, the fertilizing force of the wind. Its essence is the movement of Spirit as it penetrates into form to enliven, purify and inspire."

The Mayan Oracle - Return Path to the Stars

~ Ariel Spilsbury & Michael Bryne

Let's explore the meaning of Ellie's statement in her soul myth when she said, "I give you my many winds." According to ancient Yogic teachings, humans can attain spiritual realization by synchronizing the body and mind while meditating on the illusory or subtle body. In traditional Hinduism, humans are thought not only to have gross physical forms, but a series of energetic psycho-spiritual subtle bodies, each having increasingly sophisticated metaphysical meaning. The basic aspects of the invisible, spiritual body are called nadi, prana, and bindu.

The Yogic system of India describes this subtle physiology in terms of a series of channels or nadis, comparable to the meridians in acupuncture. The channels convey life force (prana) through the body, also called winds. The divine energy flows through three main nadis: Ida, Pingala and Sushumna. The Ida channel carries life force in the left side of the body. Pingala carries it in the right side. Sushumna, the most important channel, carries it up and down the middle of the spinal column.

The channels also include a number of focal points or Chakras similar to acupuncture points. The progression of prana through the main nadis can lead one to an experience of enlightenment. The Ida and Pingala nadis relate respectively to the parasympathetic and sympathetic nervous systems as well as the left and right brain hemispheres. Pingala is the extroverted, active, solar nadi, connecting to the right side of the brain. Ida is the introverted, lunar nadi, corresponding to the left side of the brain. These two channels are stimulated by different practices, including yogic breathing called pranayama. Pranayama includes alternately breathing in and out through the left and right nostrils to stimulate and harmonize the left and right sides of the brain.

In Sanskrit, Yama means self-control or restraint. It can also mean rein, curb, bridle, driver or charioteer. Any method that focuses on controlling the movement of prana in the body can be considered pranayama. For humans to learn how to control their prana is to purify the energetic system and make the mind ready to receive higher levels of consciousness.

The word nadi comes from the Sanskrit root "nad" meaning "channel," "stream" or "flow." It refers to the channels through which these subtle energies circulate according to traditional Indian medicine. Yogis believe there are 72,000 channels of invisible energy inside the body. They start from the central channel and extend to the periphery of the aura where they gradually become finer.

Life force energy functions at the extrasensory level and plays a part in how a person or animal responds empathically and instinctively. The term "inner air" also refers to the 'wind-energies' or 'psychic winds' that travel throughout the channels of the body's psycho physical system, as outlined in Tibetan Buddhism. The winds that flow through all the channels except the central channel are said to be impure and activate negative, dualistic thinking, while the winds in the central channel are called "wisdom winds". This is what Ellie meant when she said, "I give you my many winds." She was referring to her prana or life force energy.

By understanding and mastering these higher, subtle spiritual levels through meditation, pranayama, and yoga, we can learn how to manifest and control our spiritual energies. Horses also are masters of their own pranic energies. Horses and humans use visualization to direct the flow of winds in the body. A visualization for this is outlined in Chapter Fifteen. The general principal is that each level of manifestation is determined by ever more subtle levels of energy. The higher levels are ultimately determined at the highest position of the immortal or God.

When we are obsessed with anxiety, fear, worry, and self doubt, these become our center of gravity. They hold us down and lower our vibrations until we address and release them. The effort to compensate for our neuroses saps our joy of living and the energy for spiritual evolution. In this state, we often seek to replace the work we need to do to develop an authentic center of gravity by following a master or guru. But, we soon find out that nothing external to ourselves is really helpful.

The Tantric-Holographic Universe

According to Tantra, a branch of Eastern Indian spirituality that dates back to the 5th through the 9th century AD., the entire universe is a manifestation of pure consciousness. One aspect of this consciousness is called Shiva. Shiva is the masculine aspect with an unmoving quality. Shiva is identified with unmanifested consciousness. It has the power to be but not the power to become. The other aspect, Shakti, is the feminine aspect, the energetic and creative aspect. She is the Great Mother of the universe. From her womb, all forms come into being. Shakti relates to the Moon Goddess that Ellie introduces in her soul myth.

Tantra teaches that all life is a reflection of the universe---worlds within worlds, universes within universes: The universe as a hologram. All that is in the cosmos is found in the individual and vice versa. The same rules that apply to the universe apply to the individual. In Hindu spirituality, Shakti encompasses the potential spiritual energy that rests coiled up at the base of the spine called Kundalini. One of the objects of Tantra, and the force behind Shakti, is Kundalini yoga. Kundalini yoga awakens our cosmic consciousness and teaches us how to be one with it.

Once aroused, Kundalini unites above the crown of the

head with Shiva, pure consciousness. This union has another benefit---the resolution of duality into unity and the fusion of the individual with the Absolute. The goal is spiritual perfection. Once we achieve unity with the divine, we may control our own energy fields, as well as the forces of nature.

Through yoga, we can activate Kundalini. Likewise, the goal of the equestrian is to unite the mind and body with the horse. However, as any rider knows, this is not as easy as it seems. Just as a student of Tantra can spend a lifetime training to master the practices of Kundalini yoga, an equestrian can spend a lifetime mastering the art of horseback riding.

Within Tantric practices there are many different levels for balancing and uniting Shakti and Shiva. Each one leads to unique experiences. Some paths focus on the acquisition of worldly possessions, while others focus on enlightenment. Some place emphasis on rituals, while others employ yogic techniques. Others employ visualization and concentration. Some Tantric practitioners use herbs to accelerate their awakening, while others work with the breath. All Tantric paths and practices have one common theme: The acquisition and conscious recognition of spiritual power. It is the power to awaken fully to the wisdom and compassion within the human heart.

The power to be and the power to become, the power to grow and the power to blossom, the power to explore boundless creativity and the power to manifest it—these are the benefits of Tantra. Rising above limitation to gain access to the will, the power of knowledge, and the power of action are its goals. The term Tantra reveals how to earn access to this unlimited field of power.

Tantra is a compound of two verbs, *tan* and *tra*. The verb *tan* has two meanings. The first is "to expand, grow, expound, or give meaning." Tan also means, "to weave, intertwine, integrate, connect, or breathe newness into the old--to pull the present out of the past and give it a meaningful future." The second verb in this compound, *tra*, means, "to protect, free from sorrow and help one move away from affliction." Tantra points toward the path of health, healing, science and spirituality. It shows us our soul's purpose and helps us to weave the tapestry of life. It shows us how to protect and nurture each other and ourselves. In another sense, Tantra means the scripture by which the light of knowledge is spread. Tantra molds the power of creation and ego into skillful means. Cutting through delusion, it requires careful preparation.

The principle of integration lies at the core of Tantric philosophy. It refers to the integration of worldly endeavors with a spiritual path, to integrate good and evil, the sacred and the mundane. These harmoniously coexist within the Tantric world. Following the principle of integration, a Tantric practitioner can find redemption while living a mundane existence.

Working with horses helps humans to realize our ability to use, and misuse power. According to Sams and Carson, authors of *Medicine Cards,* those who have Horse as their totem are working with power issues, (Solar Plexus Chakra.) "The horse is physical power and unearthly power. In Shamanic practices throughout the world, Horse enables Shamans to fly through the air and reach heaven. Once humans climbed on Horse's back, they were free and fleet as the wind. Black Stallion said, 'I am from the Void where Answer lives. Ride on my back and know the power of entering the Darkness and finding the Light.' Compassion, caring, teaching, loving, and sharing your gifts, talents, and abilities are the gateways to power."

Self-Realization through Energy Awareness and Control

How can the study and practice of Tantra help equestrians understand the powerful spirit of the horse? Simply, by allowing the mind to be more like the wind, free flowing and open to spirit, we can experience the invisible forces guiding and inspiring us. Horses are also aware of their own spiritual energies flowing through their subtle bodies. Prana is the energy, or "wind" that we all use. Without these winds, yogis say our bodies would not function at all. The goal of Tantra is to awaken and harmonize the male and female aspects within ourselves---to awaken us spiritually and to realize the universe is an expression of the Cosmic Mother, the divine life force. Breathing deeply and consciously is the key to unlocking the spiritual truth of the subtle body.

Buddy made a simple reference to "the winds" in the Introduction when he said, "Every breath we take is a communication with the air. What would the air want us to know about our bodies? Where is the air stuck inside us? Where does it sense we need more of it? What does the air want us to know about its relationship with us? If we follow the path of air into our bodies and personify it, give it a voice, we will find the information it has to share with us."

In *The Collected Works of Chogyam Trungpa: Journey without a Goal*, Trungpa notes that a metaphor for prana is "a horse looking for a rider." Prana is the horse that rides the channels (nadis) in the body. The way these winds move throughout the body alters the state of mind of the practitioner and affects a horse during riding. Using yoga and meditation, a rider can gain control over his or her own mind and body and control the flows of energy that ultimately benefit a relationship with a horse.

As mentioned earlier, there are seven major vortexes, called Chakras that connect up and down the spinal column to form the Chakra System. Becoming aware of the Chakras and what they control further allows a rider to control the prana riding the channels. It is prana that connects the body at the level of the spine to each of the Chakras. If a person is blocked in one or more of the Chakras or channels, he or she will have physical trouble in that area of the body. A horse can also mirror this blockage to you. Unfairly, however, horses are often blamed for mirroring what a person is unconsciously projecting as blocked energy.

Nadi Knots

Chakras deliver life force to the physical body. This same life force helps us to heal when things get out of balance. However, stress, trauma, illness, negative emotions, and the processes of daily living can create third dimensional "knots" in our miraculous spiritual energy system. The energies of positive and negative emotional memories from childhood, held within the Chakras, also result in blocking the flow of energy through these channels. When these energies are blocked or have a low frequency for a long time, they can cause physical and mental disease.

The knots are like junctions in the path of life force that restrict the flow of prana. These kinks in the flow can be released using sound, specifically harmonic overtones. Trained yogis can "hear" the sound of their own bodily functions to resolve knotted prana by using the appropriate vibrational antidotes. Tibetan Singing Bowls are one of the sound healing tools that yogic healers employ for this purpose.

Bindu

In Sanskrit, Bindu means spot or drop. It is a term used to denote the subtle energy whose physical manifestation is identified with semen. The drops of subtle energy are located in various parts of the body and are pulsed throughout the subtle energy channels during meditation to generate the bliss associated with enlightenment.

Tibetan Buddhists tell us "bindu rides the horse of prana." Bindu refers to the spiritual consciousness that uses (rides) the breath (prana) to circulate life force through the channels (nadis). Bindu is the gathering point for meditation, contemplation, and prayer. It is the integral part of most of the mystical meditative traditions of the world. Bindu is internally experienced and conveys the highest principles and practices of yoga. In the book *The Tantric Cookbook of Nini Tantrini,* author Nancy Gorglione notes that "the nadis are prana-light paths while the bindus are points or spheres of light that travel along the pathways. The bindus travel through the nadis as radiating points of light." They are pulsed through the channels by waves or sound vibrations called bijas. Bijas are often the vehicles of esoteric transmission of terma to a tertön. Terma, (mentioned in Chapter Four) is defined as an object, text, or teaching hidden by the spiritual masters of one age for the benefit of future generations. Those who find hidden termas are called tertöns. In Hinduism and Buddhism, the Sanskrit term bîja means seed. Bija is a metaphor for the origin or cause of things and relates to the seed sounds or vibrations of the Chakras.

Understanding the End of the Journey

By utilizing nadi, prana and bindu, and by gaining control over them, we can quicken our understanding of the essential nature of the mind. According to Swami Jnaneshvara Bharati, author of the book *Bindu: Pinnacle of the Three Streams of Yoga, Vedanta and Tantra,* "Bindu is sometimes compared to a pearl and relates to the principle of a seed. There is a stage of yoga meditation in which all experiences collapse, so to speak, into a point from which all experiences arose in the first place. The bindu is near the end of the subtlest aspect of the mind itself, after which we travel beyond or transcend the mind. It is the doorway to the Absolute. Bindu guides the journey. These principles are essential in understanding advanced meditation. The experience of bindu is an inner awareness of how the highest principles and practices of yoga converge. Seeking to experience the bindu creates a focal point for yogic practices, which are intended to lead us to a direct experience of the divine."

The purpose of controlling the movements of the energies that flow within us is to gain the most profound awareness of what Buddhists call the *Bliss and Clear Light of Mind.* This inner knowledge helps to dissolve the emotional clinging and longing that destroys our peace.

Nadi, prana and bindu are also components of what Buddhists call the vajra body. Vajra is an ancient Sanskrit word for indestructible, as in the qualities of a diamond. It expresses the nature of continuity and of being ever-present and dependable. It is what Buddy described in his Soul myth as being an ever-dependable cornerstone in the Tibetan Buddhist Monastery. It comprises the qualities of sharpness and directness, like the energy and brilliance of a thunderbolt.

Vajra simply means clear determination and strong willpower. It cuts through all obstacles toward enlightenment. The vajra body is a representation of the unconditioned union of opposites and is the ultimate expression of wisdom and compassion. Buddhists have a saying, "Mind consciousness rides the Windhorse of prana on the pathways of the nadis, and bindu is the mind's nourishment."

Yoga of the Horse

"Breath is the bridge which connects life to consciousness, which unites your body to your thoughts."

~ Thich Nhat Hanh

In Ellie's Goddess Myth, she describes how a rider unites in body and mind with the Goddess of the Horse. Ellie talks about how a horse and rider can achieve perfect harmony, i.e., mental and physical union through conscious breath work and balanced posture. Learning Yoga of the Horse is a natural method for practicing concentration on our physical and mental abilities. Yoga teaches us how to recognize our unbalanced posture and shallow breathing and how to correct them even before we get on a horse.

A horse reacts quickly when a rider falls out of grace and loses the connection or "flow" that comes from a still mind. Horses respond to our false thoughts with their own brand of instinctive awareness and distrust. We cannot

blame a horse for mirroring us when we are unconsciously out of alignment. On the other hand, a balanced, confident rider can create a balanced, confident horse. That is the goal of Yoga of the Horse.[6]

The word Yoga means to "unite" or "join" various aspects of ourselves that may seem or feel separate, but which are not. It also means to "yoke." Yoga is a method of working with each level of our being individually, and unifying the levels to their original wholesome state. In Sanskrit, the word Yoga stems from the root "yuj" which refers to the processes or practices of Yoga and means the "goal" itself. The goal is also called Yoga. As the goal, the word Yoga is virtually the same as the word Samadhi, or "deep transcendent realization of the highest truth or reality."

Further, Yoga is the control, regulation, mastery, integration, coordination, stilling and quieting of the mind steam. When a person abides in him or herself and rests in his or her own true nature, this is called Self-realization. At other times, when we are not practicing Self-realization, we may take on the identity of our own false thoughts and allow these ideas to appear real. By doing so we allow false ideas to guide us into various delusions. Horses reflect both states of mind to us when we are riding. What a rider learns in the yoga studio can be transferred to the saddle.

For example, if either horse or rider ceases to flow harmoniously with the "breath" of the other, both experience a subtle loss of balance. The lack of coordination is immediately felt and reflected in the body posture of both. Before each can gracefully regain balance, they must first regain their unity

---

[6]Windhorse is an ancient symbol of the freedom and energy of our own intrinsic nature according to Buddhism.

through the flow of the breath. As noted, the yogic practice of breath control is called pranayama. Once this flow of deep breathing resumes, perfect posture resumes, and horse and rider can start over from this place of oneness..

The posture for the Yoga of the Horse is steady and balanced, as well as free flowing and comfortable. The 'stillness in motion' of yoga equals the 'effortless effort' of riding. This means perfecting a posture that is neither too relaxed nor too strained. It means allowing the rider's attention to merge with the attention of the horse. From this place of mindfulness of breath and posture, for horse and rider, a sense of freedom can be enjoyed.

Once the rider has achieved a balanced seat, a slowing down or braking of the force behind the breath can be accomplished. This breaking allows both the horse and rider to experience a steady flow of energy, that is beyond or underneath inhalation and exhalation, and the transitions in-between. Inhalation and exhalation lead to the absence of the awareness of both. In pranayama, there are three aspects of exhalation and inhalation. The third is the absence of the breath during the transition between inhalation and exhalation.

Through pranayama, the veil that masks our inner light diminishes and the mind develops the fitness, qualification and capability for true concentration. A rider needs to practice these skills first on the ground, as it is obviously more difficult to learn breathing techniques while riding a horse. The following explanation by Swami Jnaneshvara may help you to visualize the power behind pranayama.

"Like waves and the ocean: Imagine that you are sitting at the ocean, just where the waves come ashore. When a wave comes, it washes over you and runs up the beach. Then, the wave turns around, and recedes over you, going back to the ocean. Then, the current turns again, and another wave washes over you. Repeatedly, you experience this cycling process. This is like the breath, which exhales, transitions, inhales, transitions, and then starts the process again. However, imagine that you swam away from shore some distance, and dove down to the bottom (wearing your scuba tank). There, you would sit on the bottom with no waves coming or going. You might feel a gentle motion, but very slight; you are beyond, or deeper than the surface motion of the waves. So it is also with the breath."

The next time you are in a pasture with horses, take a few deep breaths and soften your vision to perceive the pranic energy field or aura surrounding each horse. You will notice several bands of colored light waves that extend from each horse's body. This is the energy field you "see" with your inner senses not your eyes. Horses use this pranic energy field to communicate telepathically with each other, other animals, and the surrounding environment. It is this auric field of energy, a synthesis of color, light, sound and spirit that connect along the spine to the Chakra system. All living beings have this energy field surrounding their bodies. This is the field of light that we access when we intuit the thoughts and feelings of nonhumans during a telepathic communication. It is the place where horses access our energy field as well.

Horses are experts at reading energy. Their lives depend on it. They demonstrate the ability when we move something in the barn or pasture and they immediately respond to the change with amazement, sometimes fear. I have

188

seen it many times with my own horses. Being able to read the aura allows us to become more consciously aware of spirit, ours and theirs. It gives a horse a chance to facilitate the process with us. Horses are intuitive beings who are helping humans to become aware of the transformation of our own consciousness.

Movement: Energy in Motion

According to the yogic theory Ellie alludes to in her myth, movement is behind all subtle energy. This includes the energy behind walking and riding. To witness the active senses in daily life means, for example, when walking or riding, one can observe, "I am moving." It is not just seeing that "I am walking or riding," but going one step further inward to observe the process of moving itself. Movement is behind or underneath the process of walking, dancing, running, or riding.

As you observe different actions and different ways of moving, you can become aware of the underlying processes behind all motion. When we want a horse to move forward, our outward actions must be accompanied by the aid of our mind and spirit. To be aware that spirit is also moving within us is an important aspect of riding a horse. The prana that moves along the pathways (nadis) of the subtle body communicates our spiritual awareness to the horse. This deeper communication originates from the aura, and includes the mind, breath, and spine. We often expect a horse to reflect our intentions accurately without realizing that we may not be clearly intending our own inner movements through our auras.

In her book, *Song of the Spine*, author and chiropractor, Dr. June Leslie Weider notes the science of chiropractic is founded upon tone. When the spine loses its "tone", the result can be what doctors call subluxation. Dr. Weider believes that each vertebra of the spine has its own frequency and that the harmonics embedded within the spine can lose their healthy resonance. In yogic traditions, the tone is called an "un-struck melody" because it is a vibration that carries energy. When the tone in the spine diminishes, Weider restores it using tuning forks. She does this much the same way a piano tuner tunes a piano. She calls her practice *bone toning*.

The idea of bone toning can help riders to better understand that the "song of the spine of the horse" must match or at least harmonize with "the song of the spine of the rider." We must realize that each one has their own specific song, which can also be out of alignment and in need of tuning. If two out-of-tune spines come together physically, the result can be discord. The discord can come from either or both. However, the discord is often blamed on an undisciplined horse.

Comparable to tuning forks, sound healers also use Tibetan Singing Bowls to realign and balance the physical energies of the body and mind. These methods are invaluable if practiced by an experienced professional.

As athletes, horses and humans need to focus on their spinal health for a good riding experience. The body/mind connection is a powerful aspect of success in any sport. In *Zen & Horseback Riding: Applying the Principles of Posture, Breath and Awareness to Riding Horses,* author Tom Nagel explains the location, importance and uses of the human psoas muscles for horseback riding.

The psoas muscles are the deep core muscles in people that link the upper body and lower girdles of the body. They are the "missing link" that a rider must learn to use to follow the directions of a riding instructor and to feel a horse's

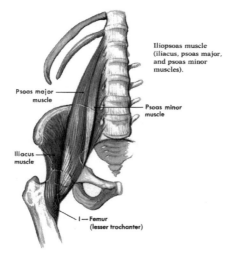

Iliopsoas muscle
(iliacus, psoas major,
and psoas minor
muscles).

Psoas major
muscle

Psoas minor
muscle

Iliacus
muscle

I—Femur
(lesser trochanter)

movements." Nagel further explains, "The psoas muscles are the only muscles that directly link the spine to the legs. They attach to the top of the inner thighs from the lower spine. Balanced flexion of the psoas muscles enables a rider to tone the inside of the upper thighs and to follow the movement of the horse with his or her pelvis. By mastering the use of these muscles, riders are able to maintain self-carriage, both on and off the horse."

The Goddess of Beauty and Movement

According to Ellie, in a conversation about beauty with author Dawn Baumann Brunke in her book *Animal Voices: Telepathic Communication in the Web of Life,* Ellie notes, "Beauty is a flow, a current that carries the wave of truth and light. . . Beauty is tied to Goddess (Kundalini) energy, for it is about expanding and elevating your frequency. . . It is the movement of Beauty that allows humans (and other beings) to connect to the divine. How does Beauty relate to the Goddess, to the divine? We will invoke the energies of inspiration; a bubbling up of ideas, a rush of emotions, a flood of feeling, a rising of passion, the union of active and passive, yin and yang, male and female. In preparing for the future Earth, we (group of Light-Beings)

191

would like to inspire the element of Beauty, not only as a tool for manifestation, but as a bridge to the divine."

It was some time after Ellie and I had finished writing "The Goddess and the Horse," that I began to understand that the Goddess in Ellie's myth was a reference point or metaphor for the Goddess energy of Kundalini. Kundalini as the Great Mother Goddess is the living energy that makes itself known to those who seek to know her. Kundalini is a powerful force and can only be approached with humility and respect. This also applies to the way a good rider approaches and rides a horse.

Although the divine is without gender, the "Goddess" in this context refers to the feminine aspect in both males and females. Ellie refers to the Goddess of the Horse as she meets the rider at that place of contact---the spine.

The Sanskrit texts speak of Kundalini as being "coiled up" three and a half times around the linga, the "sign" of Shiva. Kundalini means "she who is coiled." The coiled and dormant feminine energy refers to the vast potential of psychic energy contained within us all. It is symbolized as a serpent with its tail in its mouth, spiraling around the central axis (sacrum) at the base of the spine. The awakening of this serpent and the manifestation of its powers is a primary aim of the practice of Kundalini yoga. The awakening of this powerful energy is also the main benefit of practicing Yoga of the Horse.

However, as the powerful energy starts moving within you as you ride, it can also start to push on blocked and repressed emotions that need to be consciously released. Some riders may find that letting go of these emotions can be difficult because the emotions seem not to be under our conscious control. Consequently, for those readers who are interested in the psychology of Kundalini yoga, I recommend,

Yoga & Psychology: The Evolution of Consciousness by Swama Rama, Rudolph Ballantine, MD, and Swami Ajaya, PhD. I also recommend *Evolution in this Lifetime: A Practical Guide to Kundalini and the Chakras,* by Genevieve Lewis Paulson.

Section 4

The Mythic Threshold:
Discovering Your Soul Myth

CHAPTER FIFTEEN

The Power of Story:
Finding Your Authentic Voice

"You are now asked to go back home again. Like concentric bowls, fitting one inside the other--home is your seed essence, home is your habitat, home is your planet, home is your spiral galaxy. When you journey back home, you go into the wellspring of your power."

The Spinning Wheel

~ Gwendolyn Endicott

Everyone has a story to tell. Every being has a kernel of truth inside of them that when bathed in the light of loving intention, grows. H. G. Baynes notes this in his book *Mythology of the Soul*, "The individual's myth is defined as a stream of living images enfolding the naive mind as a river contains a trout. Akin to the trout the myth is already flowing, like a natural fountain out of the Unconscious before the human mind has a chance to set itself to the labor of thought."

The most loving communications I have had with animals happened because I asked the animals to tell me a story about themselves. This opened my mind to them, and their minds to me. From this place of openness, we touched each other at the center, at the "heart" of things. Each of us not only expands during this experience into pure being, but also undergoes an exhilarating feeling of creativity. Afterwards, lives are changed by the fleeting glimpse of how divine love flows through each one of us.

As I began to write this chapter, I asked Ellie to explain why everyone benefits from writing their own personal soul myth:

Our purpose is to unite the soul, to anchor the soul, and the body, to the Earth with our divine purpose. To know our divine purpose is to know how to serve the good of the whole.

Stepping Into the Scene

In this chapter, we will embrace the divine connection that humans share with the spiritual energies of animals not through riding, but through writing. Engaging your favorite animal (living, or in spirit) in writing your soul myth will help prepare you to open to your own form of unconscious spiritual healing. These "inner truths" within us are not found in books or taught in classrooms. They are found within our hearts and souls.

To start, you will be given steps for "grounding" to prepare for the process of writing. To "ground" means to open your "root" energy through deep breathing and relaxation, and to heighten your awareness of the pulse of the Earth. The root center of the First Chakra in the physical body has the same vibrational frequency as the Earth. When your energy is relaxed and flowing in your Root Chakra you feel at home and connected to your power.

If you are wondering how writing your soul myth can help you to learn more about communicating with nonhuman nature, here are a few of the benefits:

1. You will learn more about your soul purpose on Earth with your beloved animal(s).

2. You will deepen awareness of your own spiritual gifts when you engage animals and nature in your creative processes.

3. You will learn how to recognize and change old patterns of behavior regarding yourself and animals, and elevate your attitude toward the natural environment.

4. You will see what destructive patterns are affecting you and why it is important to "reboot" your mental and emotional systems at certain important times in your life.

5. You will reconnect to the realization and inspiration of your divine Self.

Finding Your Vibrational Signature

"It is never too late to become the person you might have been."
~ George Elliot

The Hindu mystics believe that the primal word vibrates as the sound AUM. From this initial vibration a cascade of vibrations began that fractured the One consciousness into smaller forms called "Sol" or "Soul."

In our own ways, each of us is a special soul because no one else exists exactly like us in the universe. Just as we have a unique name on the Earth, we also have a unique spiritual name as our vibrational "signature." No two souls have the same name or "signature." It is our own authentic voice that we discover when we write our soul myth.

Soul Work

Just as the total nature and makeup of the ocean can be seen in a single drop of water, so too within each of us we find a holographic image of the entire universe. In other words, each of us is an individual "drop" of living light that makes up the universal sea of starlight.

Soul is synonymous with your light body, consciousness and intelligence. Your light body is neither separate from the rest of the world, nor is it in a vacuum. You are related to every other part of the whole. The individual's soul begins with little sense of separation from the whole that surrounded and permeated its awareness in the womb. This is the fundamental experience of "being" (Shiva) before "becoming," (Shakit). When you begin writing your soul myth, you will be activating the evolutionary process of your own soul's identity or "becoming."

How to Begin

In 1987, when I was studying the Chakra System with Rosalyn Bruyere at the Healing Light Center in Los Angeles, we were given an assignment to write a personal soul myth. I wrote about riding a white horse into the center of a ceremonial fire and returning, to everyone's delight, with valuable information for my tribe's healing.[7]

---

[7] The *White Horse of the Shamans* on the book cover illustrates the horse of the ecstatic Shamanic journey in my soul myth.

198

At that time, I did not know that I was describing a Shamanic journey in what is called nonordinary reality. It was not until five years later, when I met Penelope Smith, a leading pioneer in Animal Communication that I began to put all the pieces together. I attended a Basic Animal Communication Workshop at Penelope's home in Pt. Reyes, California. It was then that I experienced my first real Shamanic journey in an exercise to retrieve a power animal for a fellow student. From there, I started to read books about Shamanism. Later, I met and studied with Dr. Michael Harner, a widely known American anthropologist who is credited with bringing core Shamanism to the Western world.

After my first workshop with Dr. Harner, I began to practice journeying with other students. In a short while, I was teaching my students how to journey to get in touch with their power animals while learning about Animal Communication in my classes.

By "dialing in" to your power animal in a Shamanic journey, you can receive greater clarity on your spiritual path of learning to communicate with nonhuman nature. It is always up to you how you use these tools to fine-tune your experience. However, if you consistently set your sacred space with love and positive intention, you will begin to gain confidence. You will begin to learn to trust the information you are receiving from your animal, and that the information is not a projection from your ego or personality self.

Power animals are our tour guides in nonordinary reality. In Shamanic cultures, it is believed that we all have power animals who act as our guardian spirits. Our power animals represent our strengths, our qualities of character, our power. In the book *Animal Speak: The Spiritual & Magical Powers of Creatures Great and Small,* author Ted Andrews notes, "The early priest/ess-magicians would adopt the guise of animals, wearing skins and masks to symbolize a reawakening by endowing themselves with specific energies. They performed rituals in accordance with the natural rhythms and seasons to awaken greater fertility and life." Ted Andrews teaches us how to connect with our power animals on his three-hour CD called, *Animal Speak: Understanding Animal Messengers, Totems, and Signs.*

Letting Go, Allowing the Flow

Although I did not know the power behind my soul myth when I first wrote it, it foretold a vitally important truth for my spiritual path. In this way, my myth was a valuable story because it represented the conscious contact I had achieved with my soul's work. It was my soul talking to me about my life's purpose--past, present and future.

My myth represented a hero's journey. According to Brown and Moffett in *The Hero's Journey: How Educators Can Transform Schools and Improve Learning,* "a hero is anyone who transcends the norms of a group to embody the highest moral virtues shared by the members of that group."

The authors state, "The hero begins in a state of innocence and unconsciousness, and ends in a state of grace and higher consciousness. The hero shows, throughout the transformation process, a sustained commitment to those ideals, which represent the best to which anyone in the group can aspire to attain."

According to Joseph Campbell in his book, *Hero with a Thousand Faces,* the adventures of the hero describe the universal journey we all take in life, and that myths are potent spiritual and psychological metaphors for healing during the

200

journey. The hero's journey follows the mythological path from immaturity to freedom--the inner struggles that lead from birth to a spiritual rebirth, and to understanding the essence of life.

In your soul myth, YOU are the hero who becomes transformed. Joseph Campbell notes, "The adventure of the hero represents that moment in life when we achieve illumination...and find the road to the light beyond the dark walls of our living death." Campbell goes on to say:

"In other words, to grow as human beings, we need to accept the call of our own life's journey. As a hero or heroine, we need to view change as a necessary thing to overcome life's ordeals. Heroes are enlightened and willing to embrace change through their expeditions. It is not society that guides and saves the creative hero, it is the other way around. And so, everyone shares the supreme ordeal--to carry the burden of a redeemer--not in the bright moments of the tribe's greatest victories, but in the silence of our own despair."

In my initial assignment to write my soul myth, Rosalyn Bruyere gave one instruction for the journey. She said that when writing a soul myth we need to write continuously by putting pen to paper, without looking back at what we have written, without editing, critiquing, rethinking, rewriting, revising, modifying, or making any corrections.

The intellect does not drive the process. It is a process of opening to your higher self and allowing that connection to take control of your creative work. The material does not come from the conscious thoughts of the writer. The story, the symbols, and the metaphors come from the unconscious mind. The same applies to writing a myth with an animal, as told to you.

Absorbing Color, Immersed in Energy

I remember writing my myth as I sat alone on my bed one afternoon. When I was finished, I was amazed at how quickly and easily it had evolved for me.

For this exercise, I asked Ellie to prepare a guided visualization to help you get started. The purpose of the meditation is not to force the manifestation of your psychic powers, but rather to prepare the ground of your being to allow the seeds of your inborn powers to bloom--Shakti style.

In a quiet, comfortable place, where no one will disturb you, sit with a pen and paper and completely relax. Take a few moments to become aware of your breathing. Then, begin by immersing yourself in the colors of the rainbow one at a time. (You may invite your animals by immersing them in the colors with you.)

Begin to absorb the colors of the rainbow one at a time, from the ground up into your feet, through your legs, and through your body to the top of your head. Start with the color red. See your body filled with a clear, bright red light at your Root Chakra (pelvis.) Bring this red energy around and through your body completely up to your crown. Next, see yourself immersed in a clear bright orange. Infuse your body with the color and allow the sensations of being touched by the color and frequency of orange to regulate your frequency. Continue following this visualization process progressively through the colors of the rainbow, red, orange, yellow, green, blue, violet, and white. To finish, immerse yourself in a clear, balanced brilliant white light. Then, you will be ready to begin writing.

Now ask your spiritual guides, angels, animal totems or whatever sacred guidance you are comfortable with to tell you a story . . . The Story of Your Soul.

When you start the process, ask to hear and record your story in childlike innocence. Then, sit and let words, pictures, feelings, sensations, visions, colors, sounds, and other imagery unfold in your mind's eye. Listen and capture these impressions on paper. Do not worry if you become startled by an image or begin to doubt. If something sounds or feels off, out of place, or uncomfortable, suspend judgment. Simply continue to write until you finish the story. The story may not make sense in the moment, but if you trust the process, you will not be disappointed.

As you get into the flow of writing, continue to breathe normally. You will need to remind yourself to stop worrying and allow the words and images to come through without internal criticism. The inner critic will undoubtedly come to the surface, as well as the ego. If you stop to read what you have written you will lose the thread of the story. If you do not understand what you are writing, do not be concerned. It will become clear in time. It is a process of discovery and the deeper meanings will be revealed to you after you have finished. It will be easier if you follow these guidelines. It goes quickly. For my first soul myth I wrote ten, hand-written pages in an hour before realizing what had happened.

When you finish writing, set the whole thing aside and walk away. Do not reread it yet. I did not look at mine again for several days. When I picked it up, I read it with fresh insight. If you have questions after reading it, sit down and ask your higher self for clarification by asking specifically about the things you do not understand. Do not dwell on it, however. Allow yourself to hear your guidance in that same "flow experience."

Visualization for Awareness of the Subtle Energy Field

Sit calmly and allow the mind and heart to let go. Begin to sense the life force within your being and gradually, through imagination and feeling, direct this life force to rise up your spine as white light, from the tail bone into the neck and then into the forehead.

When you have gathered this life force in your forehead or third-eye, direct the life force to move out from your third eye to form a body of light and energy four feet in front of you. The body of light in front of you will become dense and expand until it is as large as your own body.

Then conduct your love toward the body of light which is a profound representation of your soul's core. After a few minutes, ask the light and energy to carefully return through your forehead down into your body again to the base of your spine. Through this exercise, you will feel an accelerated renewal and spiritual awakening. You will become aware that your life force, your essence, is truly divine.

Listening to Your Higher-Self or Soul Essence

In 1957, when Carl Jung was eighty-one years old, he undertook the telling of his own personal myth in a book titled, *Memories, Dreams, Reflections*. In that book Jung notes:

"My life story is a story of the Self-realization of the unconscious. Everything in the unconscious seeks outward manifestation, and the personality too, desires to evolve out of its unconscious conditions and to experience itself as a whole. I cannot employ the language of science to trace this process of growth in myself, for I cannot experience myself as a scientific problem. What we are to our inward vision, and what we appear to be, can only be expressed by way of myth. Myth is more individual and expresses life more precisely than does science. Science works with concepts of averages, which are too vague to do justice to the subjective variety of an individual life."

In the following story, Ellie's gives further advice for connecting with the *inner child of innocence* in order to help you write your soul myth:

In creative acts of play, the child invokes the God/Goddess within him or herself. This is where all children connect at the soul level, where the soul begins to teach the child. This is true for all species on Earth, not just humans.

When a baby is engaged in "deep play", his/her mind comes alive and the heart opens. The body follows the act of what it sees, hears, tastes, smells and touches. God/Goddess interacts physically and spiritually with all life on Earth through these entryways. It is not as complicated as we might think.

To activate, in "deep play," one of the physical senses, is to engage the higher self and invite its participation into our lives. The five senses inform us of the level to which we are attuned in the moment. If a child is connecting all his/her senses to the heart and mind, we say the child is grounded, balanced. . . in a word, happy.

If the child finds delight and pleasure beyond normal sensory input, this feeling can become a pathway for the child to learn how to control his/her five senses from a higher level, for a higher purpose. The child then develops his/her extrasensory perception. The purpose for this extra sensory awareness, however, is totally unknown to children at the time, but they do it anyway. It is often difficult for adults to engage in simple acts of play when we mature because adults tend to depend a great deal on the use of logic. We think we need to have a practical purpose for everything that we do and find it difficult to let go of this concept.

To develop extrasensory awareness in children is to open them to genius, to brilliance, to flow experiences, to love, joy and healing. They make contact with their inner God/Goddess. This is a lifelong path and needs to begin early in Earthly beings.

As for young horses, we are taught to listen carefully to every sound in nature above all of our other senses. Human-made sounds are less valuable to us, and often we fear or shun them. We hear all bird songs, and Earth songs, seeds cracking open, and grass growing under our feet. The leaves blow their songs into the breeze. These things are like a symphony of love to a horse, and we cherish their continued effects on Earth.

We would preserve these sounds for our future children as they hold the deeper messages that humans cannot hear, have tuned out, or have filtered and shut out. Just think if the leaves could speak to you now. Ask a child to begin learning the language of the trees, the clouds, the water and streams. Rivers flow over rocks and they talk to you as they go. Go within to know how the blood flows through the rivers of your body and listen to it talking.

Not all life has to be audible. Many in nature talk in silence, like a bird talking to the wind with its wings held high, stretched out over the flow of air that carries it from one tree to the next. Once you are familiar with the ways of nature, from observation and personal interaction, you will become less intrusive, less disruptive. And, the children will learn from you how to allow nature to teach them about the nature inside of themselves.

CHAPTER SIXTEEN

:)

Interpreting Your Soul Myth

"All mythologies give us the same essential quest: You leave the world that you are in and go into a depth or into a distance or up to a height. There you come to what was missing in your consciousness in the world you formerly inhabited. Then comes the choice of either staying in that place with the gift you have received, or of bringing it back with you and trying to hold on to it as you move back into your social world again."

The Power of Myth

~ Joseph Campbell

In order to gain the deepest meaning from your soul myth, you will need to highlight the metaphors, images and symbols in your story. Then, using a dictionary devoted to traditional and contemporary symbolism you will need to look up the meaning(s) of each symbol. In the bibliography, I have listed several dictionaries that I recommend for this section.

Author, Jack Tressider explores core symbols across global cultures in his book *Symbols and Their Meanings*. "Every symbol bears an elemental power that transcends boundaries and holds significance for many cultures. But, the way in which we interpret these symbols varies tremendously around the world and throughout the ages."

Since symbols predate writing as a way of communicating bigger ideas, we can see them across the world, carved, painted, or worked into effigies, clothing and in ornaments. These symbols were forged for magical purposes, to ward off evil or to entreat the gods. Symbols exert their power over societies and hold us together communally. Symbols inspire our devotion and respect, or our hostility and fear. A well-balanced system of energetic symbols can also create harmony within communities or even within the larger cosmos. Symbols inspire collective action by encouraging people to fight and defend nations under their emblems, banners or flags.

Symbolism reflects the whole, the totality of meaning. Meaning is simply intuited through feeling or upon reading the symbols in writing. Symbols are not intellectual references. We perceive them through our intuition by allowing them to bypass the reasoning brain and go straight to the "knowing" brain. This is what I like to call the "mother brain."

Symbolism represents patterns, whole sequences, and the interaction of parts in full context. Therefore, it will not help in understanding them if we dissect them or cut them into little segments. They can only be integrated into the psyche as an entire unit, as a complete story or myth. The imagination fills in where things may seem unclear. The child within us brings a myth into our consciousness with a full-bodied interpretation.

Tom Chetwynd notes in *Dictionary of Symbols*, "Life in its purest form is experienced as a unity: Every twinkling star is part of a child's experience. It is only the intellect that separates the person from a star by two thousand years. This tends to alienate us from each other and the Earth. But, symbolism reestablishes contact on a grander scale by putting us in touch with a light that shone two thousand years ago, many millions of miles away."

The basic idea here is that myths cannot be understood in isolation. They are more easily comprehended as groups wherein patterns, recurring elements, and shared features link one myth to another. Myths are better understood when they are grouped into an entire mythic system.

Carl Jung saw the ancient gods as archetypes of human behavior and saw mythology as the personification of "subconscious" forces at work within the human psyche. Jung also said that besides unconscious memories from an individual's past, we have an additional universal source of unconscious information---the collective unconscious. On his internet site, Russ Dewey notes, "The collective unconscious might be described as patterns that are in the unconscious because of evolution, rather than because of the individual's experience." Carl Jung described the collective unconscious as having "unconscious images" of the instincts themselves.

This is one of Jung's most original contributions to psychology. "Underneath the surface of the modern mind" Jung says, "lurks the original mentality of our ancestors complete with vivid stories and symbols that have a natural appeal and appear unbidden in our dreams and fantasies."

The collective unconscious shows itself in patterns called archetypes, which are mostly symbols of common human social realities. These can be seen as heroes, maidens, babies, or animals, etc. Jung wrote, "archetypes are projection-making factors in the brain. To project is to see something in the outside world when its actual source is inside of you." Jung believed that archetypes are instinctive patterns in the brain that lead us to see certain patterns in people and events.

Besides giving a voice to the depths of our inner worlds, myths can connect us to things in our unconscious minds, things of which we are unaware. When we are unconsciously living a myth, rather than a life, it means that our unconscious content is "living" us. An example of an unconscious myth can be as simple as racial prejudice or a fear of spiders, and/or as complex as murder and terrorism.

If one is unable to reflect in any quiet way at all on their own life experiences, the door can close and we can become "locked in" to a restricted field of vision. The power of personal mythology lies in our ability to open these doors again, and move past the sense of being locked in place. The process of myth making is the process of finding "the way" through the light of our own higher consciousness.

Everyone loves to tell stories. We are forever constructing stories as a form of communication. We ask, "What happened," and we answer because we love to shape stories around experience. The story of our lives is our living myth. Yours and mine. These are all integrated, in connection-- small pieces to the larger puzzle of life.

In the later stages, life becomes more mythic. People seem to enjoy looking back as they get older and spinning tales about their lives becomes more natural. Every time we retell a story, it evolves a little bit. Telling stories and myths is one aspect of healing unrealized creativity. Creating personal mythologies not only creates meaning for us and our children, it is a way to celebrate and share our lives with each other.

We know that animals have innate wisdom about life. When we have the courage to listen within we can share this innate wisdom with animals. Our animals validate this when we meditate and they come to sit quietly next to us. Animals are often gifted teachers and facilitators of human transformation. Let your animals come sit by you as you write, read and interpret your soul myth. They may be able to offer valuable insights. Animals are skilled at sensing any small shift in energy in their environment. And, because of this inborn sensitivity, they can quickly respond to the inner experiences of those around them. Animals often mirror human emotions and thoughts, both conscious and unconscious. When I bought a piano recently, I found all my animals came into the room when I was playing to help me celebrate.

Is it time to contemplate your life's story? Animals and nature can help you become quiet, listen, and continue without fear so that you can write the myth your soul wants to tell. Joseph Campbell reminds us to "Read myths. They teach you that you can turn inward, and begin to get the message of the symbols. By reading other people's myths, you can begin to interpret your own."

In the next section, we are going to learn how to become more receptive to receiving communications from animals through a series of guided visualizations. These exercises require that you relax and let go. So, have fun and enjoy. Once you gain the confidence to listen to your animals, their stories will change your life, as my animals have changed mine.

"When you find yourself with the Beloved, embracing for one breath, In that moment you will find your true destiny. Alas, don't spoil this precious moment. Moments like this are very, very rare."

From *Thief of Sleep* by Shahram Shiva

Section 5

Growing Your Potential For

Animal Communication

Through Love, Joy, Compassion,

Equanimity, and Peace

CHAPTER SEVENTEEN

Guided Visualization and Meditation

What is Guided Visualization?

Visualization is a tool we use to improve mental clarity, focus and concentration. Through mental imagery, we can redirect our energies to intended, often spiritual, goals. Using imagination to "sense" a scene, person or object, with intense clarity, we can concentrate on attaining a specific outcome. Often, we achieve this through guided visualization when we enter into an imaginary space and time where we make personal, inner discoveries. Visualizations performed by a trained hypnotist are a proven and effective method for affecting the processes of body, mind, and spirit.

In the modern view of "world as hologram," where everything is a projection of consciousness, it becomes clear that each of us is more responsible for ourselves than our current wisdom allows. What we view as miraculous remissions of disease may be due to changes in consciousness which in turn effect changes in the hologram of the body. Similarly, the healing techniques used in visualization may work so well because in the holographic domain of thought, mental images are ultimately as real to the brain as our current perception of "reality".

Even visions and experiences involving "non-ordinary" reality become explainable under the holographic paradigm. In his book *Gifts of Unknown Things,* biologist Lyall Watson describes his encounter with an Indonesian Shaman woman who, by performing a ritual dance, made a grove of trees instantly vanish into thin air. Watson relates that as he and another astonished onlooker watched the woman, she caused the trees to reappear, then "click" off again and on again several times. Although this ability may confound hard science, experiences like it are more believable when "hard" reality is only a holographic projection.

Perhaps as a culture we all agree on what is "there" or "not there" because what we call *consensual reality* is created and confirmed at the level of the unconscious mind where we are infinitely interconnected. If this is true, it is the most profound implication of the holographic paradigm, for it means experiences such as Watson's are not commonplace only because we have not programmed our minds with beliefs that make them so. In a holographic universe limitless possibilities exist for us to alter the fabric of our lives.

What we perceive as real today may only be a canvas awaiting the visualizations that extend our consciousness. Anything is possible, from bending spoons to the events Carlos Castaneda experienced with don Juan. Magic is our birthright and no less miraculous than the ability to create our own reality in the dream state.

What is Meditation?

Meditation includes a diverse assortment of techniques that cultivate mindfulness, concentration, tranquility, and insight.

214

The techniques of core meditation have been preserved for thousands of years in ancient Buddhist texts through teacher-student transmissions. The closest word for meditation in the classical texts is bhâvanâ, which means to "make grow" or "to develop." Buddhist meditation has become so popular in the West today that many non-Buddhists are learning the benefits of these techniques in order to cope with the stresses of modern culture.

Meditation can also be used as a method of healing through total absorption on the purest energy source in the universe. This is the mana of the Polynesians, chi of the Chinese, ki of the Japanese, prana of the Eastern Indians, baraka of the Muslims, num of the Kalahari bushmen, manitou of the Algonquian Indians, and the force of Obi Wan Kenobi.

We can sense prana by turning the mind inward and listening to the inner source of sound, to the source of inner light, or illumination. Trance-inducing repetitive chanting, drumming, mantras, mandalas, or chanting a seed sound, all enhance meditation practice.

Exercises such as Yoga, tai chi, breath work (Pranayama) and guided visualization are all forms of concentration that can fill the body and mind with light. Meditation aims at slowing the processes of the mind in a natural way, by deeply relaxing the body and maintaining the mind in a neutral state of emotional and mental detachment.

A meditator can maintain this state for a short time or a few hours, depending on his or her skill level. Purity of intention is achieved during meditation and is essential for accessing the higher self. The higher self does not admit the impurities of the ego. Meditation is necessary to achieve a state of perfect balance and composure, called equanimity.

Your higher self is the perfect spiritual form of you.

The inner voice of the higher self gently guides you on your journey through life. This guidance may manifest in subtle ways through words, pictures, images, as flashes of insight, or through intuition and sudden knowing.

Spiritual energy flows throughout the universe as light, sound and color. It fills the body and mind during meditation. The many other not-so-absorbing activities of daily living can allow for absorption, or meditative stillness, but, they are often too monotonous for us to become fully absorbed in them. The awareness achieved during meditation is called "extension of consciousness," "expanded awareness," "trance state," or "alternate state of consciousness." In Shamanism, it is a "state of ecstasy."

In the following visual journeys, you will enter into meditation through the gateway of your higher self. This gateway allows you to access your meditative, inner silence. By practicing silence, breathing and stillness, you can achieve anything you set your mind to do. You glimpse this state when you have a concentrated focus, an open heart, detached emotions, and wholesome intentions. Inner stillness is a safe place where the mind and soul can meet in harmony and self-acceptance.

When we perceive images, through the third eye, the mind awakens to the symbolic language of the soul. The pictures we perceive during visualization are the result of the mind's eye becoming activated through suggestion. In the meditative state, a deeper dialogue occurs between the higher self and the person.

The following guided visualizations are a series of spiritual journeys that will take you to a place where all things are possible. In the King James Version of the Bible, there is a passage that explains: "The light of the body is in the eye:

216

Therefore if thine eye be single, the whole body shall be full of light." Matthew 6:22.

The main purpose modern people seek to meditate is to see with a "single eye." In the West, we meditate to dissolve the frenetic energies that constantly vie for our attention. We are neurotic without silence and stillness. The West is a continuous, outwardly focused culture with many electronic devices---televisions, telephones, computers, radios, fax machines and cell phones. These devices can bring the outside world "in" to us. But, there are no devices that can bring the inner world "out" of us, except prayer and meditation. The best way to do this is to recognize and communicate with the soul through the spirit. That is to say, the spirit guides us through our endeavors while connecting us with our soul. We can accomplish this through dreams, meditation, prayer, sacred art, dance, music, Yoga, and in visualization while reflecting on the source of our inner strength.

In meditation and contemplation, the soul enters into communion with the higher self and gives us a glance at our fullest potential. As we discover our fullness, bit-by-bit, we realize there is only one true soul, one true purpose—and that we are an integral part of that truth. I believe there is no separation between my soul and the soul of other beings. We are made of the same "soul stuff," with individual personalities, expressing the same divinity, like a many-faceted jewel.

Before practicing the following exercises, please read them through first. Then, practice each one in the order it is presented. When you finish each one, record your thoughts in a journal for future reference.

As you practice, you will become more comfortable with the effects of contemplation and meditation and derive more pleasure from the mundane activities of life as well. In the future, you may want to dedicate a part of each day for practicing quiet stillness. Typically, thirty minutes, day and night, is enough for maintaining a meditation practice.

If at first you experience resistance, continue to practice. Working through your resistance and coming back to your focus are important aspects of practicing meditation. You will be able to still your mind and experience the grace and peace that silence and stillness bring after you have been practicing for a while. One time my cat told me, "I am in a state of perfect grace, and peace is all around me." She was suffering from cancer at the time and close to death. But through meditation she was able to maintain peace of mind.

Eventually, the ego, which causes resistance to spiritual practice, will fade and the barriers will come down. If you work through the resistance, you will be able to walk the Middle Path. The Middle Path in Buddhism refers to the practice of being neutral and centered. It means to search for the core of life and all things with an unbiased view. In order to solve a problem, Buddhists teach us to position ourselves on neutral and unbiased ground. From there, we can investigate a problem from various angles, analyze the findings, understand the truth, and reach a reasonable conclusion. A direct experience of meditation allows us to understand the importance of these practices for mental and emotional health.

Hundreds of books have been published about meditation. But, the principles are the same: Relax the body, become aware of your breathing, concentrate your energy on one central theme or point within, or without, and center your awareness on the stillness between breaths. Once you are comfortable, begin to expand your energy and awareness beyond the confines of ego and slowly identify with a greater whole, family, community, country, nation, universe.

After meditation, you may wish to ground the energy and expand the experience into projects and activities in the everyday world by putting into action what you have learned. If you wish to go deeper into the practice of meditation, you may want to find an instructor in your local area.

Step One: The Practice of Self-Illumination

Between the moments of stillness and silence and the many activities of daily living, there is a deeper awareness we call consciousness or self-awareness. This conscious awareness helps us to achieve the things we have always dreamed of doing. When we discover the true nature of the mind, we can let go of all concerns and relax into it. In other words, we can rest in our own basic, true nature. In this context, mind refers to our inner essence.

As discussed in Chapter Fourteen, according to advanced yogic teaching, in the illusory body, mind-consciousness rides prana (literally, "wind" or breath). The prana travels on the pathways, called nadis. The bindu ("drop," as in Ellie's dewdrop portal) is understood as the mind's nourishment as the result of the two brain hemispheres being synchronized. When they are not balanced, it signifies that we are caught up in the duality of subject and object, "this and that."

When body, speech and mind are precisely calibrated these emerge in their indestructible (vajra) diamond-like, natural state. When we have synchronized the body and mind through yoga, or any balancing work, the practice of meditation becomes easier. The method I recommend for the following visualizations is to include them with the practice of yoga. Take your time to learn yoga from a professional instructor. And, once you have practiced for a few months, the ability to communicate with nonhuman nature can emerge effortlessly.

Step Two: Awareness is Key

In the following pages, we will explore the gateway to inner stillness. Inner stillness can most easily be glimpsed or sensed with a disciplined, quiet mind, open heart, and detached emotions. Inner stillness is fundamental to a thriving psyche. When we see inwardly, we can perceive the metaphoric language of the soul. This metaphoric language employs symbolic imagery to communicate in our dreams and visions. Then, we need only to learn the meaning of the symbols and metaphors to make sense of the message.

Step Three: Begin by Slowing Down

The main purpose for slowing down is to become conscious of the breath. As you advance you will become more absorbed in the practice of Pranayama and want to dedicate more time to it each day. As you take what you have learned from meditation into the world, your relationships with animals and nature will be enhanced. By bringing your inner light out, you will touch those in your life more deeply. Animals, friends, family, neighbors, all will see you in a "different light." The only caution, which is the same for starting anything new, is to be patient with your progress. This is a gradual and gentle awakening, one that takes time and patience.

Meditation One

Receiving the Gift of Telepathic Animal Communication

Close your eyes and let your whole body relax. Sit with your spine erect in a chair or crossed legged on the floor on a cushion. Rest your open palms on your thighs. If using a chair sit with both feet on the floor. Relax all the muscles around your head, face, neck and shoulders. Let your mouth open slightly as though you are holding a piece of paper.

Enjoy the peace between each breath. When thoughts intrude, let them float away like waves in the sea. Once your body is completely relaxed, you are ready to begin.

Imagine you are walking on a quiet country path at sunset. Orange and red sunlight glints through the rustling leaves of a Maple tree. The sunlight warms your skin and feels soothing. You rub your hands together briskly and cup your palms to your eyes. This feels restful and you are content.

As you walk, you see many magnificent things. A sparkling stream flows quietly beside you. If unwanted thoughts intrude, place them into this stream and watch them drift away.

When you come to a clearing in the forest at the edge of the meadow, a deer and her fawn glide quietly past. As you continue, you notice a forceful stream of air escaping through a small burrow in the ground. You go over and see the spot where the air is the strongest. You then discover an opening in the ground.

You clear away some stones to find a passageway that looks like the entrance to a cave. What is beyond the opening is hardly visible, but the hole is big enough to peer inside. As you do, you decide to climb down through the hole into the cave.

Once inside, it becomes dark quickly. However, you can see a light flickering at the far end. You move deeper into the dark chamber, toward the light. You realize the cave is ancient. Perhaps many millions of years ago great Spirits once lived here.

After walking farther from the entrance, you notice a brilliant, twinkling star on the roof of the cave. It illuminates the ceiling, floor, and walls.

Now, the chamber opens up and you see everything more clearly. The beauty and majesty of the rock formations are amazing. The knobby surfaces of the walls create different dancing apparitions, and colorful reflections, even shimmering effects. You extend your hand to touch the massive structure and as you do some shadows emerge to form animal shapes on the walls.

In front of you stands a huge, black bull, a perfect image of strength and confidence. Other images start to form: horses with well-defined manes and tails, in absolute reality. Elephants, elk, bison, mammoths and other primitive creatures come to life before your eyes.

These images stretch up to cover the ceiling surrounding you overhead. The horses face you with broad black contours and brown patches suggesting three-dimensional shapes. One tosses his head with a fiery snort. You realize this place is home to many sacred energies.

Some of the animals you already know. You feel their strength as they come alive and jump off the walls. They begin to fill the room with their primal energies. A drum begins beating slowly in the background.

You watch as the animals dance around you.

Suddenly, one of the horses comes down off the wall and stands in front of you. You feel the animal is a friend, she looks and feels familiar. You sense this animal has been expecting you. Below, at your feet, you feel the rocks are moving and there is a buzzing in the air.

You are fascinated by the animal's strength, beauty, form and movement. It is an animal you have dreamed of in the past. The animal also may be a beloved childhood friend. Its powerful spirit inspires awe. It is such a delightful being that you cannot resist her powerful attraction.

You allow the animal to lead you into a playful dance as you begin leaping and twirling around. The animal gestures for you to follow the movements. Soon both of you are whirling and spinning in an ecstatic dance. You are light and every movement is performed with effortless joy. You keep time with the heartbeat of the Earth. You feel your own heart beating faster and although the animal does not speak directly to you, you know she is asking you to follow her.

She challenges you to move deeper into the cave with her. You glance at the cathedral of rocks on the ceiling. This cave is a picture gallery covered with a complex of ancient animals. The colors are rust, red, brown, black, and tan. You squeeze through narrow crevices around sharp outcroppings. You crouch to crawl through small openings, following the natural bulge of inner Earth you come out in a different place.

You think you have lost contact with your animal when suddenly you see each other again. You stand in a chamber with a high-domed ceiling. The ceiling is so high you bend your neck to see to the top. This hall has seen many ceremonies in the heart of the Earth. Your animal appears and leads you to the center of this majestic and spiritual stone temple.

Once in the center, your animal calls you by name and gestures to sit on the floor next to her. The room fills with light as words are forming across the rocks. A moment later, you can hear these words whispered into your ear.

Love, joy, compassion, peace.

As you listen, you recall pleasant memories and experiences of each word's meaning for you in relationship to animals. LOVE . . . JOY . . . COMPASSION . . . PEACE.

The words now merge into a swirling ball of white light. Your animal takes this ball of light, puts it into a small box and closes the lid. Then she gestures for you to put out your hand. As you do, you take the box and hold it close. Slowly it melts into your Heart Chakra.

Your animal then speaks and you know it is a message you will remember. After listening to the message, your animal finishes, saying:

"These qualities are inside you; these qualities make you human. As your friend, I want to help you to expand the qualities and bring them to life so that you may express your fullest potential."

You thank your animal for this gift, and pause in a moment of silence. When you are ready, you follow your friend back out into the light again.

At the gate to the outside world you say goodbye. But you promise to meet again. Then, slowly you open your eyes, take a deep breath, and allow yourself to return to the room.

To remember everything you have just done, you will need to record your experiences in a journal for later reflection.

Meditation Two

Growing Your Potential for Animal Communication through Compassionate Action

"The root seed of all and everything is compassion. Make every effort to activate this precious inner potential."
~ Longchenpa

The focus of the following meditation is to release the preoccupation humans have with the self, and to reconnect with an animal in a new way through compassionate action. This allows greater understanding of another species by letting go of human-centered awareness. It also provides an avenue for developing relationships with totem animals. It allows exchanging self with other and, for feeling another being from the inside out.

The power of movement provides a graceful vehicle for dancing the essence of other species. Dancing embodies the essence of life itself. As the breath moves rhythmically in and out, it breaks down emotional blocks, and allows us to feel and release them. Anyone can dance an animal because there are no steps. When we move or dance to imitate animals, we help our bodies adjust to the vibrational frequencies of that animal.

Dancing an animal is older than Yoga itself. Animals have inspired many Yogic postures. The postures are actually named after animals. Isadora Duncan once noted in her autobiography, "How beautiful these movements are that we see in animals, plants, waves and winds. All things in nature have forms of motion corresponding to their innermost being. Ancient humans still have such movements and from that point we can create a beautiful movement that sets itself in harmony with the motion of the universe. I never taught my pupils steps. I never taught myself technique. I only told them to appeal to their spirits, as I did to mine."

In dancing our totem animals there is no choreography. There is only the union of soul and personality. That is when the dancer leaves off and becomes the dance.

As humans, we crawl, walk, run, jump, leap, spin, twist, bend, and kneel. Still, there are many creatures with many more legs than ours or none at all. Moreover, it takes imagination to experience another species in this way.

To walk, think, feel and see from inside a cat, dog, bee, butterfly or ant is what every child dreams of, at least until this wonderful activity is frowned upon later in life and replaced by more "grown up" activities.

Once we have learned compassion we can realize what our animal's want and need from us. This is an important step in communicating with another species. Animals need quiet time too and they may not immediately interact with us. But for the most part, when we are meditating, our animals sit with us because they also enjoy sitting in silence as much as we do.

For this meditation, you will need to find a quiet place. Close your eyes and let your whole body relax. Sit with your spine erect in a chair or crossed legged on the floor on a cushion. Rest your open palms on your thighs. If using a chair sit with both feet on the floor. Relax all the muscles around your head, face, neck and shoulders. Let your mouth open slightly as though you are holding a piece of paper.

Enjoy the peace between each breath. When thoughts intrude, let them float away like waves in the sea. Once your body is completely relaxed, you are ready to begin.

Choose an animal friend to work with for this meditation. Imagine yourself in your animal friend's habitat or environment. If a tiger, go to the jungle, if a whale, go to the ocean, if a dog, imagine the dog in the backyard. Whatever the habitat is imagine you are in the middle of it.

Once you can see your animal's habitat, imagine the sounds, smells and other life forms living there. Begin to call out softly (in your mind) to your animal friend. You can do this by using a name you create, or by visualizing the animal coming into your field of vision from a distance, perhaps from behind a tree or a rock.

Once you see your animal in your mind's eye, align yourself with him or her by imitating their movements and behavior. Imagine they are engaged in finding food or playing with other animals. Perhaps they are sleeping in the grass. Whatever the animal is doing do that now.

When you feel comfortable mirroring the actions of your animal, begin to imagine yourself as the animal's offspring. Shrink yourself down to the size and shape of a baby animal, like Alice in Wonderland, or grow yourself up big. Become young and dependent and in need of nurturing.

How does this feel? Notice how the mother feed her young. Does the father participate in raising the babies? Do your parents mate for life? What food are you eating? Are you nursing from your mother? If not, what method does she use to feed you? Are you taught how to seek out and perhaps kill food on your own yet? Or, do you wait for food to be delivered? Are you hungry now? What are your parents doing? Do you have siblings?

Begin to see yourself living as one of the flock, herd, pack, pride, school, etc. Where are you living? Are you in a lair, nest, tree, bush, water, or underground? What does it feel like?

227

How do your parents help? Are you licked and groomed? Feel this and take a few minutes to immerse yourself fully in the experience of loving kindness.

Now take a few moments to experience your animal guiding and teaching you the skills of survival. Do all the young go on an adventure into the woods? Perhaps you are following the tail of your brother or sister in front of you. Where does it lead you? What lessons are you going to learn today? How do you learn, by observing, doing, making mistakes? Observe the lessons now.

How do your animal parents lead you away from danger? How do you interact with animals of other species? Whatever your new parent asks you to do, do you do it? Are you fun loving? Or are you serious? Whatever you are like, you know you are loved, accepted and cared for. Feel this and know it in your heart. Experience this at a deep emotional level. Become the love you feel. All of this communicates the most wonderful loving kindness and compassion that exist in the universe. There is nothing more important than the loving attention of parents and these loving emotions. It is the essence of our being. It is the essence of compassion. Take a few minutes to know the protection, love and nurturing your parents are showering upon you. This is a beautiful gift.

Meditation Three

Growing Your Potential for Animal Communication Through Love

"His ears were often the first thing to catch my tears."
~ Elizabeth Barrett Browning, (referring to her cocker spaniel.)

Universal love is unique and cannot be duplicated. It is one with All That Is. To know universal love is to grow like a rose. To communicate with an animal through love you will begin by choosing an animal that you love for this visualization. In doing so, you will find your own way according to your own needs. The following guided exercise lays the emotional groundwork for opening you to your inner wisdom.

For this exercise you are asked to imagine yourself in partnership with an animal, seeking to complete and understand each other, rather than judging and controlling. See his or her spiritual essence and merge with it completely, mind, body, and soul.

Close your eyes and let your whole body relax. Sit with your spine erect in a chair or crossed legged on the floor on a cushion. Rest your open palms on your thighs. If using a chair sit with both feet on the floor. Relax all the muscles around your head, face, neck and shoulders. Let your mouth open slightly as though you are holding a piece of paper.

Enjoy the peace between each breath. When thoughts intrude, let them float away like waves in the sea. Once your body is completely relaxed, you are ready to begin.

Imagine an animal you would like to communicate to in a loving way. It is through this trust and innocence that the animal comes into your life. Imagine asking the animal to teach you, through trust, how to find your innocence and sense of delight and wonder in the world. Take a few minutes to allow the animal to come to you. It may be a wild animal or an animal you know. The animal is completely open, agreeable, and willing to communicate in a friendly manner. If the animal is not friendly, go on to a welcoming animal instead.

Now see yourself on a plateau overlooking the ocean with the animal. Glints of sunlight reflect on the water below, filling your whole being with love and warmth. The ocean gently rocks back and forth on the shore as seagulls swirl overhead. The sky is bright with fluffy, white clouds.

You are sitting with your animal looking out at the expanse of ocean. Allow your heart to open, sit back and open your chest. Your mind is clear of all cares and worries. There is no sense of separation between you and the animal, the ocean, and sky.

Feel yourself blending into one. Your souls are connecting as one soul with the expansive sky and ocean. You begin to listen without fear or judgment to what your animal wants to tell you. You are free to connect and it feels wonderful. Now face your animal and hear the song in his or her heart. How does it uplift you? Is there something more your animal wants to share with you? Take time to listen carefully and open to receiving the communication in the spirit of love. If you have questions, you may ask now. Sit still knowing this expression of love is the best kind for all beings. When you are ready, open your eyes and write down what you experienced in your journal.

What is a Lov-er
By Buddy and Dr. Jeri Ryan

A lov-er
Is anyone who commits to love.
Love asks the lov-er to step outside of themselves,
To step outside of me,
And bring my thread so it will be our own special kind of love.
Love takes not my desires,
But, allows them to melt away

230

So as not to be so cumbersome.

Love allows me to silently, and without taking up space,

Be within the one I love so as to understand what love will serve them best.

Love is free and open and boundless, and has no price.

When one has given love one can turn ones back,

Because there are no expectations of a return.

A true lov-er has no I-ness.

A true lov-er must love the self beyond all distractions to the contrary.

A true lov-er has convictions that are undaunted.

A true lov-er loves with whatever it takes to love.

Sometimes saying good-bye from the place of love,

When goodbye brings sorrow.

Sometimes loving when love brings sorrow.

A true lov-er stops at nothing and perseveres,

And is driven by love to accomplish the love;

A love of a person, purpose, cause, group or species.

When love changes for a true lov-er, it only deepens.

A true lov-er is never disappointed.

Their love is never shaken by the foolishness, ignorance, and Naivete of the one we love.

A true lov-er has compassion for all and carries that love to the masses, herds and tribes beyond.

A true lov-er makes sacrifices for the cause of the love.

A true lov-er is never without love no matter what pain might hide it.

A true lov-er trusts that love is always there and that is what Makes us all real.

A true lov-er knows that love is what we are.

And that when we love ourselves we can only be
love to all those around us.

And we can only love all around us.

Opening to our true love.

Love goes to battle.

Love does not give in.

Love perseveres.

Love knows the truth and holds it in the face of danger or
nuisance.

Love is light and takes us to our true self and is our true self.

Love takes us to peace and enlightenment.

Love has been buried because all fear it.

We must come back to love.

We must be in our love. We must be in love.

We must be love.

Meditation Four

Growing Your Potential for Animal Communication Through
Joy

*"Joy does all things without concern. For emptiness, stillness,
tranquility, silence and non-action are the root of all things."*
~Chuang-tzu

Turning to the next meditation, you are asked to think of a
child, a joyful child you know and love. If you can remember
a time when you and the child were together in joyful play, you
will be able to do the following meditation. For it is in play that
joy finds release, through spontaneous joy and letting go of all
that binds you.

232

Joyfulness is a soft breeze blowing, dolphins leaping, puppies wrestling each other to the ground. Joyfulness fills us with limitless creative expression. Every life form plays according to its own nature. Merging with sounds, smells, air, and colors heightens clarity and joyfulness. Being in harmony with one another, being in touch with feelings and thoughts that merge, gives instant understanding and pure enjoyment.

Pure joy is knowing everything is in perfect harmony. Joyfulness does not need material props to manifest. We do not need material things to be joyful. In this meditation you will recall a time when you played joyfully in connection with another being. You played without elaborate material things. You could have been throwing a Frisbee for a dog or running on the beach. You can imagine sitting with a cat in front of a fire. The cat is crawled up, purring, keeping you warm. Animals are joyful and adaptive. They do not need anything but their bodies to express joy.

Close your eyes and let your whole body relax. Sit with your spine erect in a chair or crossed legged on the floor on a cushion. Rest your open palms on your thighs. If using a chair sit with both feet on the floor. Relax all the muscles around your head, face, neck and shoulders. Let your mouth open slightly as though you are holding a piece of paper.

Enjoy the peace between each breath. When thoughts intrude, let them float away like waves in the sea. Once your body is completely relaxed, you are ready to begin.

Recall a joyful activity you experienced with an animal friend. Relive that experience now with your friend, inviting your animal to relive that experience in your imagination. Once you have truly experienced it in your mind, write about it in your journal.

Ode to Joy
by Buddy and Dr. Jeri Ryan

Joyfulness makes me stand up on two legs and get pulled to the sky.

I float. I fly. I feel the bursting of my heart into huge music that floats far away into infinite places.

Joyfulness has power that strengthens heart and mind and body.

It stretches us to our fullest potential of love and life.

Everything is possible with joyfulness.

We see only joy when we see or have sadness.

We break through with buried joyfulness that has such power to stay alive despite squashing pain.

Once we know joyfulness, it is ours forever.

Joyfulness is also quiet and makes no sound.

It is felt within and keeps us solid.

That is more constant joyfulness.

More balanced joyfulness helps us all to know of our constant beingness.

And our closeness to being joy and being love

With joy we find love and all we need.

Without joy we are alone.

Nourish joy, find joy, keep joy.

Let it be full and part of you at all times.

When it disappears, even for a moment.

Call it back to be on the sidelines while you have pain.

Always know that pain cannot kill joy.

Pain only teaches, and does not kill.

When in pain, joy is forgotten.

Pain teaches us about joy.

Pain helps us to know the joy of resolving it.

And of accomplishing and growing.

Then, we know the joy that waits on the sidelines

Do not ignore joy.

Embrace joy at each moment and trust it.

Remember it is yours in each moment.

As long as you know it in each moment,

And stay with it in each moment. I have joy as I eat grass and as I breath in the moon, And as I sleep.

Those are my favorite joys.

Because they enter me and go deep and stay there.

I do not understand those joys,

But I do know them. No one needs to understand joyfulness.

But everyone needs to know joyfulness. Knowing joyfulness means taking it in and allowing it to become a part of your person,

With trust in its realness and in its perseverance.

Joyfulness makes love, it makes big love in hearts.

Love makes joyfulness, it makes big joyfulness in hearts.

Joyfulness makes your heart bigger.

So does love.

Together they weave an opening to the beingness we long

for and don't know because we wait for it instead of recognizing that it is here with us now.

Joy to you. Love to you. Joy in your heart,

Joy in your heart,

Joy in your heart, Joy.

Meditation Five

Growing Your Potential for Animal Communication Through Equanimity

Divine purpose and momentum are at work even in the most desperate situations. To experience equanimity is to know your core composure, especially during a crisis. The practice of equanimity does not seek to escape pain. Instead it seeks to integrate your inner potential with your outward actions. Equanimity creates inner peacefulness in the face of stress, turmoil and conflict.

An analogy for equanimity is to see someone struggling in quicksand but to have the "presence of mind" to know that if you jump in with both feet you will both go down. Equanimity stays on firm ground and maintains clarity to provide the optimum assistance to both self and other.

To be completely effective in resolving conflicts, and to maintain grace and composure, and also to help another, we must have a sense of being removed slightly from the drama. We can observe the drama but not become involved in it. We need to have compassion enough to be helpful without taking on the emotions. If we take on the pain of another without distance, the drama can incapacitate us as well.

One of the hardest things to overcome in difficult emotional times is the temptation to panic and lose our composure. We need strength in difficult times to divert our habitual negative thinking and self-cherishing minds and turn to the power of loving kindness.

When we think of ourselves too much, we have the feeling of being separate from each other. This limited idea deprives us of the ability to unite with others. In learning how to become unified in heart and mind we uplift and support other beings. The more we can maintain our equanimity, the more we can hear, feel and know the truth and the best action to take.

So, when you become aware of the habitual mind, the one that it is moving in a direction that does not reflect equanimity through a sense of composure, you need to return to the core self and refocus on a sense of peace in the present moment.

The following visualization is written to help you to become focused and grounded in your core essence: To find your equanimity.

Close your eyes and let your whole body relax. Sit with your spine erect in a chair or crossed legged on the floor on a cushion. Rest your open palms on your thighs. If using a chair sit with both feet on the floor. Relax all the muscles around your head, face, neck and shoulders. Let your mouth open slightly as though you are holding a piece of paper.

Enjoy the peace between each breath. When thoughts intrude, let them float away like waves in the sea. Once your body is completely relaxed, you are ready to begin.

Recall a time when you were with an animal that was in emotional or physical pain. You may have over-identified with the animal's pain so much so that you could not function effectively. Or, you denied the pain and became crippled with helplessness.

Because of these feelings of grief, you were unable to take the right action needed for the animal. But, realizing now that emotional paralysis limited your ability to feel and think clearly, you have pangs of quilt and shame.

Now ask yourself for permission gradually to

become centered and grounded and at peace. Remember that you are here to serve a higher purpose, and the higher purpose of the global community. With this thought in mind, it is also appropriate that animals can experience their opportunity to serve a higher purpose, and their higher selves.

While focusing on an animal's connection to his or her divine consciousness, and allowing yourself to see your higher purpose with animals, ask to see the divine lesson in the current situation when you were incapacitated. What is the lesson for you, what is the lesson for the animal?

Now give yourself the opportunity to create a different outcome from the one in which you failed to act due to being out of balance. Take your courage with a positive intention by using equanimity to return and re-experience the same situation, only this time, create a different response. Use your present awareness of equanimity. Write down the new result, if there is one, and ask a friend to go over it with you, someone who knows you and your animal intimately.

Meditation Six

Growing Your Potential for Animal Communication Through Peace

"If we have no peace, it is because we have forgotten that we belong to each other."
~ Mother Teresa

True peace can only come when we give up our defenses. When we feel we are going to be attacked we feel the need to arm ourselves. True courage to be at peace means giving up the

238

need for protection, in faith that no one is going to harm you. This kind of devotion and faith allows us to have a peaceful frame of mind that can be obtained through the practice of meditation.

We cannot hold onto anger, fear or resentment when we fully understand another being's point of view. Just as we want to be understood, we need to acknowledge and recognize other people need the same understanding. True communication fosters mutual understanding. Since peace of mind is an interior matter, it must originate with our thoughts and feelings. Then, starting with this perspective, peace can arise from the self and move out into the world. If we continue to hold onto unresolved conflicts and deep-seated grudges, the entire flow of positive life-sustaining energy becomes blocked, depriving us of our health and happiness. The following meditation will help you to create a deeper union with your inner self, and with other humans and animals.

Facing and clearing unresolved conflicts, loving ourselves and forgiveness are the prerequisites for total inner peace. As eloquently stated in the Course in Miracles, "The still infinity of endless peace surrounds you gently in its soft embrace, so strong and quiet, tranquil in the night of its Creator

In this visualization, you will get in touch with an internal conflict without being fearful or judgmental or self-critical. You will be able to release a conflict by bringing it out of the subconscious into your conscious awareness for resolution. This allows you to release the conflict and receive the triumph of inner joy.

Close your eyes and let your whole body relax. Sit with your spine erect in a chair or crossed legged on the floor on a cushion. Rest your open palms on your thighs. If using a chair sit with both feet on the floor. Relax all the muscles around your head, face, neck and shoulders. Let your mouth open slightly as though you are holding a piece of paper.

Enjoy the peace between each breath. When thoughts intrude, let them float away like waves in the sea. Once your body is completely relaxed, you are ready to begin.

Imagine you are walking alone on a familiar path in a place where you feel safe and secure. It may be a place you know, or it may be a place in your imagination. If you need to, you can imagine walking with an animal friend or with an Angel to help illuminate the way.

Create this path in your mind now. Hear, see and feel the different and beautiful sights and sounds that comfort you on the path. As you walk, you will imagine a 12-inch-thick rose tinted piece of glass as a wall that is separating you from whatever it is that you fear, cannot face easily, or are unable to accept.

This glass wall is behind you on the path. You are going to glance back at the wall to see the situation that you fear through the lenses of the tinted pink glass. You will see the situation as it completely fills your field of vision through the wall. The wall is clear so you can see through it, but it is a deep rose color.

While walking, you will casually glance backwards at the wall. Whatever you see will draw you closer. Go with it in the knowledge that doing so is safe to do. When you are ready, see whatever or whoever is on the other side. It may be further away than you think, nevertheless look until whatever is there is clear to you.

Realizing that this wall protects you, give yourself full permission to see through the wall at the situation now.

Once you have the image in your mind ask your higher self for resolution to the conflict. Listen to your thoughts and feelings. Allow yourself time to focus on the resolution and when you have finished, turn back onto the path and continue walking forward. After a few steps, open your eyes and return to the room. Write down your experiences in your journal for future reference.

EPILOGUE

Buddy's Leg-up into Heaven

It was a normal day, just like any other day. A day that Buddy would have prescribed for this event had he known what was about to take place. I was on my way to an appointment in Portland, dressed and ready to leave. Like every morning, since I can remember, I would go up to the barn to let the horses out after they had finished eating breakfast. Everything was as it should be. It was nine o'clock.

Today, something was different. A week earlier, I had started giving Buddy a prescription called Pergolide for Cushing's Disease. The vets diagnosed it ten days earlier and he was improving with the medicine. Each day, I hid the pill inside the soft flesh of half an apple. He would take it out of my hand without hesitation. Yet, today something was not right. I held out my hand to him and he did not move toward me to take the apple. I put it out again. Again, he did not move.

"Come on, Buddy," I said, noticing the strained look on his face. "Damn it." I whispered under my breath. "The Cushing's Disease has finally made him founder."

As I thought this to myself, I ran into the house to call the vet. The vet said she had another emergency and could not come until later in the day. But, Buddy could not move and I was starting to panic.

I called a friend and asked her how to check for founder. She asked me to touch his hooves for heat. Nothing. Then, she mentioned something about feeling a pulse in the back of his leg. I'm not sure now. When our conversation ended she was on her way to our house--a 50-mile drive.

When she arrived, she immediately started talking to Buddy. She looked him over and we both could not figure out what was wrong. I was in such a state of panic I could not hear him telepathically. By now his whole body was lathered with sweat.

I called the vet again and she suggested I go to the clinic and pick up a muscle relaxer called Banamine. I put some hay and water in front of Buddy, assured him we would be right back, and left the barn.

On our way home, after getting the drug, we decided to stop at a coffee shop for something to eat. As I recall this now, it seems ridiculous we would have stopped at all. But, something told me Buddy and I needed a little time to get ourselves together for what was to come.

When we drove up to the house, the vet was just arriving. Two hours had passed since I first discovered Buddy in that condition. He was standing in the same place but, he had munched a little of the hay to calm himself.

The vet started the exam. Within no more than a couple of minutes, she announced that Buddy's left hind femur was broken. He would need to be put down.

I was speechless. I could not think, feel or act. I was in shock.

I managed to get my cell phone and leave a message

for Dr. Jeri Ryan, my former mentor. She immediately called back.

"What happened?" Jeri asked. I could not say anything except to ask her to talk to Buddy about his leg and ask what he wanted to do. The vet said she could do nothing else for him and recommended that I put him down right away. This all came too soon! I did not feel I could make this decision alone.

Buddy told Jeri that unless someone could take away the pain and fix his leg he wanted to be set free. I hung up the phone and told the vet to go ahead with the euthanasia. As they prepared him for the lethal injection, Ellie started running back and forth as if she was going to jump over the stall door between them. Knowing her, it was possible. So we decided to give her a sedative. Once it took effect, I put my arms around Buddy, let out a heart-wrenching sigh and left the barn to wait in the pasture. The vet explained the drug goes straight to the animal's brain and they do not feel a thing. It would be quick and humane.

Nevertheless, I could not bear to see my horse, my mentor, my best friend for the last fifteen years, put down like this. By now he was even more exhausted. My friend offered to stay with Buddy and the vet while I went outside to call a friend in Alaska. I stood in the pasture sobbing as I told her the story. She suggested that she talk to Buddy after he passed over and she would email me later with what he said. I agreed and we hung up.

A few minutes later, I went back to the barn and found Buddy on the ground. He looked surprisingly peaceful. But still, he was gone. I let Ellie out of her stall, and she stood over him for a long time sobbing. It was the first time I had ever seen a horse crying. As she hung over him, tears fell from her eyes onto his fur which later left a stain on his cheek. She drooped over him so low that she touched his cheek with her muzzle.

I was running on adrenalin. When my friend left, my husband arrived, and I told him the news. His response was so visceral he buckled, as if someone had punched him in the stomach. That is how we both felt for the next few weeks and months as I tried to make sense of what had happened to Buddy, and why.

Later in the evening, my friend emailed the conversation she had had with Buddy. By then, emails were pouring in from around the country as friends, family, clients and students heard the news of Buddy's sudden passing. He had touched many lives in his lifetime.

The following conversation with Dawn Baumann Brunke and Buddy took place after he passed on that day. It helped those who knew him to envision the best possible ending to a life that was short, but full of love, compassion and tenderness.

[End Note]

I know readers will ask what happened to Buddy in the barn that day. Buddy had been suffering from Cushing's Disease and this condition can cause a horse's bones to weaken. Every Spring, Buddy and Ellie acted frisky with each other. On the first day of Spring in 2007, they had been what Buddy called "messing around" (his words) when he slipped, turned the wrong way, and broke his femur in the barn. I guess you can say it was a "freak accident." But Buddy says there are no accidents. He later explained to Jeri Ryan that we had come to the end of our journey. We had accomplished his section of the book, his mission was complete, he was needed elsewhere. He was twenty years old.

In our next book, *Love From the Other Side*, Buddy and I continue to write about the deepening connections of love between spirits of animals and humans, and what happens at death, and in the afterlife. The aim? To enlighten readers about the beauty and warmth of eternal love that comes from a place of mystery and awe, a place we call heaven; a place where we meet our loved ones again, when the time is right . . . when true love prevails.

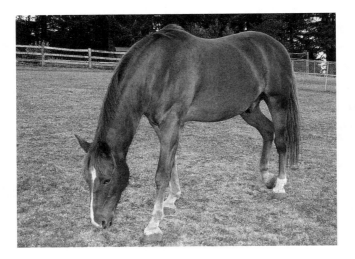

Buddy in the Summer of 2006

Goodbye to Buddy

"True love stories never end."
~ Richard Bach

Wednesday, March 21, 2007
5:45 P.M., Alaska Time
Dawn Baumann Brunke

Hi Buddy. I am checking with you to see if you have something to share with us.

I see an expansive sky, and Buddy running-flying through it. As if he is accessing many lives and rejoicing in a large sense of fullness. Like he is remembering with a fuller expression and manifestation of his Buddyness.

I feel him smiling here, telling me that my translations are uniquely mine, but they do a fine job of conveying his "joy of fullness" in being free of the body. He says this is not necessarily just him, but on leaving the body many beings feel this rush of joy in opening to the fullness of who they really are. And it is exciting to feel that--to be that—to remember that fullness.

So, this is the feeling I'm getting from him right now—such a rush of joy.

I am asking about his body as Buddy the horse. Was

he in pain, what happened? He is sidestepping that...just wanting to rejoice in this joyful feeling. He is sharing it with me—this big, open, expansive feeling of joy. It is air-oriented, full and wide. Maybe that is why I keep seeing a very expansive open sky with layerings of golden-lit clouds. He says it is there for you too. That when you are ready, you can tap into this joy and feel his release...even be there with him as he rushed out of his body and began to fly-run up into the sky. "Skyward," as he says.

Again, I feel a lot of rejoicing with other horses...ancestor horses, maybe horse selves that are also in some way Buddy, and more. I am clearly seeing Ellie and other horses, Buddy has known.

He says, "We do this both within and without bodies." He shares that horses (he isn't excluding other animals, but he is talking primarily of horses) often do feel this connection of flying into the sky, and that there is a celebration of sorts that all may participate in...whether they are in body or out of body.

He says he wants to tell you that things may be different in the barn for the next few weeks and months. He says he will visit. He will be around—you can count on that (he says with emphasis)--and that he will help with the transition, not just of his death, but of the changes his death may cause. He advises you to be still, to take time for yourself--just being, resting, meditating, walking. Not doing, but being.

Ah! He says he sends you "FLOWERS." Here he is showing me an image of you and him out in the grass, in a pasture where there are flowers, a dream image perhaps. You are by a brown wood fence. You are on one side of the fence. He is on the other. You are laughing and talking; you have a basket and you are collecting wild flowers as you laugh and talk.

248

He is eating an apple from a tree. "The tree of life!" he says, and there are all kinds of associations with that, many layers there, but he says he gives you that as an image-present for your "Mythic Mind." He says he sends it to you as a little gift, "a momento" he puts it (and he says, yes, that is both a moment ((a moment of oh!)) and a memento, as in a present to you personally).

He says he has much to share about death and dying and the death experience. I sense his joy, his overall exuberance. He says "Of course" he will come to talk to you and finish your book and work with you. He says not to doubt that for a moment, for even an instant. He will be present and available to you and others, and he urges you to be open to a new way of doing things, and that he will be close.

He sends you a warm muzzle and a closeness you know, remember and are fond of. He says he was much more to you than "just a horse"…there are many energetic relationships present here (between the two of you) and this (his death) came about as an "agreed-upon promise" between the two of you — and others. He says you may not believe this now, but "precision and timing and beneficial forces are at work here." He will elaborate more for you as you continue to release your grief and open your heart. (The last sentence, was a para-phrase of what he said in feeling-tones — and he affirms that as I read over this, yes that is correct…release grief and open your heart.)

He signs this, and he is asking me to be sure I get this exactly right: LOVE from the Wonderful World of Buddy!

Citations and Bibliography

MacFadden, Bruce, J. *Fossil Horses: Systematics, Paleobiology, and Evolution of the Family Equidae.* Cambridge, U.K.: Cambridge University Press, 1992.

Prothero, D. R., *The Eocene Oligocene Transition: Paradise Lost.* New York: Columbia University Press, 1994.

--------, *Horns, Tusks, and Flippers: The Evolution of Hoofed Mammals.* Baltimore, MD: The John Hopkins University Press, 2002.

Mellon, Nancy. *The Art of the Storytelling.* Rockport, MA: Element Books, Inc., 1992.

Larsen, Stephen, PH.D. *The Mythic Imagination: Your Quest for Meaning Through Personal Mythology.* New York: Bantam Books, 1990.

Jung, Carl. *Symbols of Transformation: An Analysis of the Prelude to a Case of Schizophrenia.* Princeton, NJ: Princeton University Press, 1990.

Pearson, Carol S. *Awakening the Heroes Within: Twelve Archetypes to Help Us Find Ourselves and Transform Our World.* San Francisco: HarperSanFrancisco, 1991.

Greene, Rosalyn. *The Magic of Shapeshifting.* Boston: Weiser Books, 2000.

Trungpa, Chogyam. *Crazy Wisdom.* Boston: Shambhala Publications, Inc., 1991.

Sams, Jamie & Carson, David. *Medicine Cards: The Discovery of Power Through the Ways of Animals.* Sante Fe, New Mexico: Bear & Company, 1988.

Von Rust, McCormick, Adele PH.D., McCormick, Marlena Deborah, McCormick, Thomas E. *Horses and The Mystical Path: The Celtic Way of Expanding the Human Soul.* Novato, CA: New World Library, 2004.

Broersma, Patricia. *Riding Into Your Mythic Life: Transformational Adventures with the Horse.* Novato, CA: New World Library, 2007.

Kohanov, Linda. *The Tao of Equus: A Woman's Journey of Healing & Transformation through the Way of the Horse.* Novato, CA: New World Library, 2001.

--------, *Riding Between the Worlds: Expanding Our Potential Through the Way of the Horse.* Novato, CA: New World Library, 2003.

Keen, Sam & Valley-Fox, Anne. *Your Mythic Journey: Finding Meaning in Your Life Through Writing and Storytelling.* Los Angeles: Jeremy P. Tarcher, Inc. 1989.

Feinstein, David, PH.D., & Krippner, Stanley, PH.D., *The Mythic Path: Discovering the Guiding Stories of Your Past–Creating A Vision For Your Future.* New York: A Jeremy P. Tarcher/Putnam Book, 1997.

Eliade, Mircea. *Shamanism: Archaic Techniques of Ecstacy.* Princeton: Princeton University Press, 1974.

--------, *Images and Symbols: Studies in Religious Symbolism.* Princeton: Princeton University Press, 1991.

--------, Mircea Eliade, *Yoga, Immortality, and Freedom.* Princeton: Princeton University Press, 2009.

Greene, Liz and Sasportas, Howard. *Dynamics of the Unconscious: Seminars in Psychological Astrology, Volume 2.* York Beach, ME: Samuel Weiser, Inc., 1988.

Schmidt, Jeremy. *In the Spirit of Mother Earth: Nature in Native American Art.* San Francisco: Chronicle Books, 1994.

Tresidder, Jack. *Symbols and Their Meanings: The Illustrated Guide to More than 1,000 Symbols—Their Traditional and Contemporary Significance.* London: Duncan Baird Publishers Ltd., 2000.

Cooper, J. C. *Symbolic & Mythological Animals.* London: HaperCollins Publishers, 1992.

Walker, Barbara G. *The Woman's Dictionary of Symbols and Sacred Objects.* San Francisco: HarperSanFrancisco, 1988.

Paulson, Genevieve Lewis. *Kundalini and the Chakras: Evolution in this Lifetime, A Practical Guide.* St. Paul: Llewellyn Publications, 2002.

Wauters, Ambika. *Chakras and their Archetypes: Uniting Energy Awareness and Spiritual Growth.* Berkeley: The Crossing Press, 1997.

Swimme, Brian and Berry, Thomas. *The Universe Story: From the Primordial Flaring Forth to the Ecozoic Era: A Celebration of the Unfolding of the Cosmos.* San Francisco: HarperSanFrancisco, 1992.

Berry, Thomas. *The Dream of the Earth.* San Francisco: Sierra Club Books, 1988.

Wauters, Ambika. *Chakras and Archetypes: Uniting Energy Awareness and Spiritual Growth.* Berkeley: The Crossing Press, 1997.

Plato. *Timaeus and Critias.* London: Penquin Books. 1977.

Cruden, Loren. *The Spirit of Place: A Workbook for Sacred Alignment.* Rochester, VT: Destiny Books, 1995.

Matthews, Boris, Ph. D. *The Herder Dictionary of Symbols: Symbols from Art, Archaeology, Mythology, Literature and Religion.* Wilmette, IL: Chiron Publications, 1993.

Shepard, Paul. *The Others: How Animals Made Us Human.* Washington, D.C.: Island Press, 1997.

Lawlor, Robert. *Voices of the First Day: Awakening in the Dreamtime.* Rochester, VT: Inner Traditions, 1991.

Thurman, Robert A. F. *The Tibetan Book of the Dead: Liberation in the Understanding in the Between.* New York, Toronto, London, Sydney, Auckland: Bantam Books, 1994.

Gold, Peter. *Navaho & Tibetan Sacred Wisdom: The Circle of the Spirit.* Rochester, VT: Inner Traditions, 1994.

Endicott, Qwendolyn. *The Art of Mythmaking.* Portland, OR: Attic Press, 1994.

Cooper, J. C. *Symbolic & Mythological Animals.* London: The Aquarian Press, 1992.

Chetwynd, Tom. *Dictionary of Symbols.* London: HarperCollins, 1982.

Walker, Barbara G. *The Women's Dictionary of Symbols and Sacred Objects.* San Francisco: HarperCollins, 1988.

Paulson, Genevieve Lewis. *Evolution in this Lifetime: A Practical Guide, Kundalini and the Chakras.* St. Paul: Llewellyn Publications, 2002.

Brunke, Dawn Baumann. *Animal Voices: Telepathic Communication in the Web of Life.* Rochester, VT: Bear & Company, 2002.

Eden, Donna, Feinstein, David Ph.D. *Energy Medicine*. New York: Jeremy P. Tarcher/Penguin, 2008.

McArthur, Maggie. *Wisdom of the Elements: The Sacred Wheel of Earth, Air, Fire, And Water*. Freedom, CA: The Crossing Press, 1998.

Rinpoche, Dagsay Tulku. *The Practice of Tibetan Meditation: Exercises, Visualizations, and Mantras for Health and Well-Being*. Rochester, VT: Inner Traditions, 2002.

Krishna, Gopi. *The Awakening of Kundalini*. Darien, CT: The Kundalini Research Foundation, 2001.

Rama, Swami, Ballentine, Rudolph, MD, and Ajaya, Swami, Ph.D. *Yoga & Psychology: The Evolution of Consciousness*. Honesdale, PA: Himalayan Institute Press, 2007.

--------, *Yoga Psychology: A Practical Guide to Meditation*. Honesdale, PA: Himalayan Institute Press, 1976.

Erdoes, Richard, Ortiz, Alfonso. *American Indian Myths and Legends*. New York, Pantheon Books, 1984.

Ocean, Joan. *Dolphins: Into the Future*. Kailua, HI: Dolphin Connection, 1997.

Diemer, Deedre. *The ABC's of Chakra Therapy: A Workbook*. York Beach, ME: Samuel Weiser, 1998.

Andrews, Shirley. *Lemuria and Atlantis: Studying the Past to Survive the Future*. St. Paul, MN: Llewellyn Publications, 2004.

Trine, Cheryl. *The New Akashic Records: Knowing, Healing & Spiritual Practice*. Portland, OR: Essential Knowing Press, 2010.

Dale, Cyndi. *The Subtle Body: An Encyclopedia of Your Energetic Anatomy*. Boulder, CO: Sounds True, 2009.

Johari, Harish. *Chakras: Energy Center of Transformation*. Rochester, VT: Inner Traditions, 2000.

Mohawk, John, Lyons, Oren, Deloria, Vine. *Exiled in the Land of the Free: Democracy, Indian Nations, and the U. S. Constitution*. Santa FE, NM: Clear Light Publishing, 1998.

Wolf, Robert. *Last Cry: Native American Prophecies: Tales of the End Times*. Santa Fe, NM: Grail Publishing, 2003.

Tobias, Michael, Cowan, Georgianne. *The Soul of Nature: Celebrating the Spirit of the Earth*. New York: Plume, 1996.

Smith, Penelope. *Animals in Spirit: Our Faithful Companions' Transition to the Afterlife*. New York: Atria Books, 2008.

--------, *When Animals Speak: Techniques for Bonding with Animal Companions*. New York: Atria Books, 2009.

--------, *Animal Talk: Interspecies Telepathic Communication*. Tulsa, OK: Council Oaks Books, 2004.

Baldwin, Christina. *Storycatcher: Making Sense of Our Lives through the Power and Practice of Story*. Novato, CA: New World Library, 2005.

Conway, D. J. *Maiden, Mother, Crone: The Myth & Reality of the Triple Goddess*. St. Paul, MN: Llewellyn Publications, 2001.

Campbell, Joseph. *Pathways to Bliss: Mythology and Personal Transformation*. Novato, Ca: New World Library, 2004.

--------, *Myths of Light: Eastern Metaphors of the Eternal.* Novato, CA: New World Library, 2003.

--------, *Hero with a Thousand Faces,* Novato, CA: New World Library, 2008.

Bierlien, J. F. *Parallel Myths.* New York: Ballantine Publishing Group, 1994.

Bierhorst, John. *Myths & Tales of the American Indians.* New York: Indian Head Books, 1992.

Von Franz, Marie-Louise. *Creation Myths: Patterns of Creativity Mirrored in Creation Myths.* Zurich: Spring Publications, 1978.

La Duke, Winona. *The Winona LaDuke Reader: A Collection of Essential Writings.* Oroville, WA: Theytus Books, 2002.

Benedik, Linda and Wirth, Veronica. *Yoga for Equestrians: A New Path for Achieving Union with the Horse.* Shropshire, UK: Kenilworth Press Ltd., 2006.

Deloria, Vine, Jr. *Spirit and Reason.* Golden, CO: Fulcrum Publishing, 1999.

Weider, June Leslie. *Song of the Spine.* Booksurge Publishing, 2004.

Fremantle, Francesca. *Luminous Emptiness: Understanding the Tibetan Book of the Dead.* Boston, Shambhala Publications, Inc., 2001.

Brunke, Dawn Baumann. E-mail correspondence with the author, January, 2002-2009.

Hadingham, Evan. *Secrets of the Stone Age.* Ontario, Canada: Beaverbooks Ltd., 1979.

HOW TO SCHEDULE A CONSULTATION

OR WORKSHOP

WITH CAROLE DEVEREUX

Daily across America the bonds between people and animals are broken because of misunderstandings about animal behavior, resulting in millions of animals being relinquished to shelters, and euthanized.

The core purpose of animal communication is to help people and animals deepen their connection, resolve their conflicts, and find a healthy balance of love and discipline. The business of communicating with animals has gone from just a few people in the 1990s to several thousand practitioners across the world in the last twenty years.

With this many people looking for ways to reduce animal suffering in the world, why not join them in learning how easy it is to bring comfort and joy to even the smallest and most helpless creatures.

Carole Devereux offers telepathic animal communication readings by phone nationally, by email internationally, and in-person in Washington and Oregon. She also travels to teach workshops.

If you are interested in sponsoring a workshop in your area, or wish to schedule a reading for your animal(s), please send an email to caroledevereux@animalinsights.com, or visit her website at www.animalinsights.com.

You can also call her office at 360-263-7268 in Washington, Monday through Friday, 8 A.M. to 7 P.M. Emergency sessions can be arranged on weekends and evenings for sick and/or lost animals by calling 503-320-2977.

[Note:] The Windhorse painting on the title page is reprinted by courtesy of the artist, Sandra Belfiore-Severson. Please see her website for more information at www.sandrasseverson.com.

The Wind Horse (Lung-ta) is the most prevalent symbol used on Tibetan prayer flags. Windhorse carries the "Wish Fulfilling Jewel of Enlightenment", representing good fortune and uplifting life force. When one's Lung-ta is low, obstacles arise. When Lung-ta is high, good fortune abounds. Raising Wind Horse prayer flags is one of the best ways to raise one's Lung-ta energy.

Buddy and
Carole in 1995

INDEX

A

B

palms, 221, 226, 229, 234, 237, 240
Pandora, 118, 120, 121
Pantheon, 254
Parahippus, 58
partnership, 76, 229
passageway, 159, 221
pathway, 103, 205
patriarchy, 139
patterns, 31, 32, 90, 106, 111, 123, 140, 197, 208-210, 256

peace, 68, 75, 87, 111, 114, 116, 127, 157, 158, 184, 212, 218, 221, 224,
    226, 229, 232, 234, 237-240
Pegasus, 139
Pergolide, 242
phantoms, 141
phenomenon, 35, 73, 171
Phowa, Tibetan, 135
Pingala. 176
Plato, 252
Pliocene, 60
Plotkin, 31
polarities, 108
politics, 34
Polynesians, 215
portal, 49, 150, 158, 159, 164, 173, 219
Poseidon, 139
power, xiii, xvii, 28, 36, 38, 42, 46, 47, 56, 71, 74, 76, 77, 85-88, 91, 104,
    112-115, 117-119, 121, 127, 129, 132, 139, 140, 142,
    147, 154, 158-160, 163, 171, 178-181, 187, 195, 196,
    199, 200, 207, 208, 210, 225, 234, 237, 250, 255
prana, 175-177, 181-185, 187, 189, 215, 219, 220
pranayama, 176, 177, 187, 215, 220
pranic, 177, 188
prayer, 41, 126, 183, 217, 258
predator, 53, 58
prehistorians, 69
prehistoric, 46, 50, 51, 54, 65, 66, 74, 75, 46, 49, 63
priestesses, 140
primitive, 46, 53, 54, 61, 64, 68, 222
primordial, 73, 76, 140, 252
prophecy, 94, 48
prostration, 166
Prothero, 250
Psalm, 36
psoas muscles, 190, 191
psyche, 5, 71, 72, 76, 88, 111, 140, 142, 170, 208, 209, 220
psyche/nature, 72
psychically, 90
psychological, 4, 165, 200, 251
psychology, 32, 192, 209, 254
puppy, 22, 63
purification, 109, 118, 119, 165, 169